Kindred
SPIRIT

BOOKS BY CATHERINE M. ANDRONIK

Quest for a King
Kindred Spirit

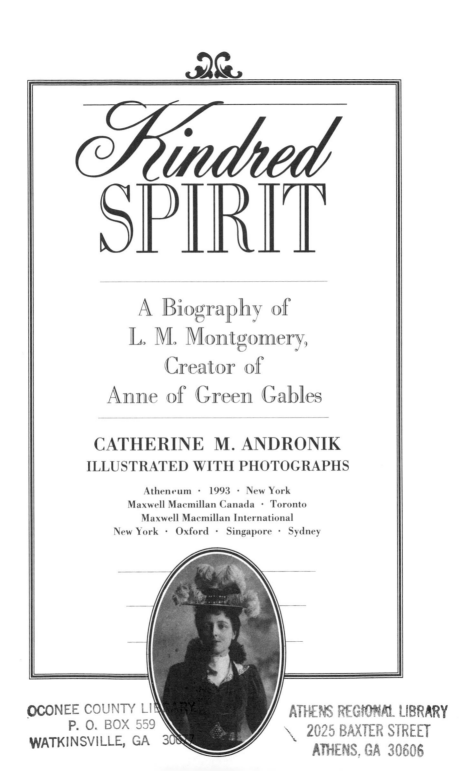

Kindred SPIRIT

A Biography of
L. M. Montgomery,
Creator of
Anne of Green Gables

CATHERINE M. ANDRONIK
ILLUSTRATED WITH PHOTOGRAPHS

Atheneum · 1993 · New York
Maxwell Macmillan Canada · Toronto
Maxwell Macmillan International
New York · Oxford · Singapore · Sydney

Atheneum
Macmillan Publishing Company
866 Third Avenue
New York, NY 10022

Maxwell Macmillan Canada, Inc.
1200 Eglinton Avenue East
Suite 200
Don Mills, Ontario M3C 3N1

Macmillan Publishing Company is part of the
Maxwell Communication Group of Companies.

FIRST EDITION
PRINTED IN THE UNITED STATES OF AMERICA
2 4 6 8 10 9 7 5 3 1

THE TEXT OF THIS BOOK IS SET IN BODONI
BOOK DESIGN BY C. MALCOLM-RUSSO/SIGNET M DESIGN, INC.

Library of Congress Cataloging-in-Publication Data
Andronik, Catherine M.
Kindred spirit: a biography of L. M. Montgomery, creator of Anne
of Green Gables / by Catherine M. Andronik.—1st ed.
p.   cm.
Includes bibliographical references.
Summary: Covers the personal life and literary career of the
Canadian writer best known for her novels about Anne, a girl from
Prince Edward Island.
ISBN 0–689–31671–2
1. Montgomery, L. M. (Lucy Maud), 1874–1942—Biography—Juvenile
literature.   2. Novelists, Canadian—20th century—Biography—
Juvenile literature.   [1. Montgomery, L. M. (Lucy Maud),
1874–1942.   2. Authors, Canadian.]   I. Title.
PR9199.3.M6Z584   1993
813′.52—dc20
92–25869

*or my mother—*
who gave me a copy of
Anne of Green Gables
when I was eleven

Acknowledgments

This book would not have been possible without the invaluable assistance of several people in Canada. Professor Mary Rubio of the University of Guelph, who has been editing the journals of L. M. Montgomery, read an early draft of the manuscript; her comments and clarifications made a great difference, especially in Chapter 10. Marion Dingman Hebb, the attorney for the Montgomery family, facilitated my use of quotations from the writings of L. M. Montgomery and personal photographs of the family. Finally, my thanks to Nancy Sadek in the archives at the University of Guelph, for patiently researching the photographs that illustrate this book.

Contents

Introduction

One day, when this book was nothing more than an idea, I was in a restaurant. At the table next to mine was a family: mother and father, and a girl of about eleven. The girl held a sandwich in one hand and a book in the other. And she was clearly more absorbed in the book than in her lunch. Finally her father asked her what she was reading. She showed him the paperback's cover—and I glanced over. The book was *Anne of the Island.* "*Another* Anne book?" her father exclaimed. "There are *lots* of them," the girl replied happily—and returned to her reading.

A few months later, walking through town, I passed a bus stop. Sitting on the bench was an older woman, just as absorbed in a book as that eleven-year-old girl had been. The cover caught my attention: It was *Anne of Ingleside*.

L. M. Montgomery created Anne, her family and friends, and her fictional home of Avonlea on very real Prince Edward Island, and later on mainland Canada, between 1905 and 1938. She wrote other stories, poems, and books as well. She was born in 1874 and died in 1942. It was a groundbreaking time in history for a woman to dream of becoming a serious writer, and to succeed. It was also a time when a book originally written mainly for children and teenage girls could become a phenomenal best-seller with universal appeal. What could have drawn a young girl into such a challenging field? What qualities made her so successful when so many others failed? And why, after nearly a century, is *Anne of Green Gables* a perennial classic, enjoyed around the world as a book, a film, a play, a musical, a television miniseries, and even a ballet?

What kind of woman was L. M. Montgomery? She was very much an individual, with strong opinions, even stronger emotions, and a heart full of hopes and dreams that sustained her through a lifetime of disappointments and hardships. She was the kind of woman who loved the poetic—"curling breakers, woods and mountains and stars and trees and flowers"—as well as the ordinary—bedtime snacks and chocolate caramels.

Maud Montgomery, with her complex personality, enjoyed a full life, a life that began on a small Canadian island, on an early winter day in the late 1800s.

Chapter 1

*J*ust off the eastern shore of New Brunswick, Canada, lies an island. Nowhere on the small island are you far from the sound or the salt smell of the sea. Its little towns are crisscrossed by paths of packed earth the color of brick and surrounded by fields of every imaginable shade of green sprinkled with lavender-colored lupines in the spring and summer.

The island was called "Home Cradled on the Waves"—*Abegweit* in the language spoken by the native people who once lived there. The French who settled there later called it Ile St.-Jean. But most people today know it better as Prince Edward Island, Canada's smallest province.

Abegweit, or Ile St.-Jean, or Prince Edward Island,

was home to a girl who also had a choice of names. That girl, who would become known to the world as the author L. M. Montgomery, had been christened Lucy Maud. She was named Lucy after her grandmother on her mother's side. Her family was patriotic, so they added Maud in honor of one of the daughters of England's beloved Queen Victoria.

The young writer-to-be was very particular about names, and always would be. Lucy Maud was never called Lucy. She insisted on being called Maud—and not *just* Maud, but Maud "spelled '*not* with an e,' if you please." Never forgetting her particularity about names, Maud would one day create a character who would state emphatically, "Please call me Anne spelled with an 'e'."

Maud lived on a farm outside the town of Cavendish with her mother's parents, Alexander and Lucy Macneill. She lived with her grandparents because her father was often away on business, and her mother was dead.

Maud's mother, Clara Woolner Macneill, had been "a beautiful, spiritual, poetic girl full of fine emotions and noble impulses." She fell in love with and married a young sea captain named Hugh John Montgomery. He gave up the sea and settled down in Clifton Corner on Prince Edward Island, not far from both his parents and hers. At Clifton Corner he opened a general store. Before long, the Montgomerys were the parents of Lucy Maud, born on November 30, 1874. But soon after the birth of her baby, Clara became ill with tuberculosis, a disease of the lungs. There are treatments for it now, but in the 1800s its victims often simply wasted away

Maud's mother, Clara Macneill Montgomery, died when Maud was just a baby.

and died, as Clara Montgomery did. She was twenty-three years old when she died, leaving a daughter not quite two years old.

Although she was very young when her mother died, Maud would always remember the sad event. At that time, instead of holding a wake in a funeral parlor, the

Maud's father, Hugh John Montgomery, was often away from his family on long business trips to the Canadian West.

coffin was set up in the family's living room, where people would come to pay their last respects to their loved one. Maud could remember her family gathered in the house for the funeral. And she could remember her beautiful mother lying still in a casket. As her father held her beside the coffin, little Maud reached out to touch her mother's face for the last time.

> Even yet I can feel the coldness of that touch. Somebody in the room sobbed and said, "Poor child." The chill of Mother's face had frightened me; I turned and put my arms appealingly about Father's neck and he kissed me. Comforted, I looked down again at the sweet, placid face as he carried me away.

For years afterward, people told Maud that her mother was now in heaven, which Maud assumed was a place, very far away perhaps, but a place she could travel to nevertheless. When she was four years old, she attended a church service with one of her aunts. Suddenly, the minister caught Maud's attention: He was talking about heaven—where, Maud knew, her mother was. So, very quietly, Maud turned to her aunt and whispered, "Where is heaven?" Her aunt did not want to talk during the service. Instead, she pointed upward—right toward the attic of the church, as far as Maud could tell. For a long time Maud believed that heaven was a room above the ceiling of the Clifton Presbyterian Church, and that, if she could find stairs or a ladder, she could visit her mother there.

After his young wife's death, Hugh John Montgomery did not want to stay on Prince Edward Island. He took a job with the government and began to travel extensively in the wide-open Canadian West. There were vast lands waiting to be developed, and the gov-

Maud was raised by her grandparents on her mother's side, Alexander and Lucy Macneill.

ernment needed men to see that all this development was being handled properly. Soon, Mr. Montgomery began to dabble in real estate in the western province of Saskatchewan. He visited his daughter as often as he could, whenever his business brought him back to

Prince Edward Island. But more and more, his real home was in the West.

So Maud, back on Prince Edward Island, was raised by her grandparents. They were both in their mid-fifties when their baby granddaughter came to live with them. They had raised six children of their own; but those children, except for one daughter, Emily, who would marry in a few years, had long since grown up and moved away. A baby in the household disrupted the quiet farm life the Macneills had become accustomed to. And Maud was no ordinary child.

Suddenly, with Maud there, everything on the farm had a name. In the orchard were trees Maud called Little Syrup, Spotty and Spider, White Lady Birch. In the yard were a maple and a spruce that had grown intertwined: The Lovers. Even Maud's potted flower was called Bonny. "I like things to have handles," Maud explained, "even if they are only geraniums."

Then there were cats and kittens—creatures the Macneills generally disliked unless the beasts were catching mice in the barn, where, according to most farm people, cats belonged. Maud, however, loved cats and always managed to have at least one as a special house pet.

Two of Maud's first kittens were called Catkin and Pussywillow. Catkin was a rather ordinary sort of cat, but Pussywillow was a perfect little kitten—and gray, Maud's favorite cat-color. Suddenly one morning, Maud found Pussywillow very sick—in fact, dying. The kitten had eaten some of the poison left around the farm to kill rats and mice. There was nothing Maud could do to save Pussywillow. She was heartbroken when the kitten died. She remembered her mother's death, but then she had been too young to understand what dying meant. Seeing what happened to Pussywillow, Maud suddenly realized that everything could and eventually would die, even innocent kittens. She later wrote in a letter to a friend: "Before that I had been a happy, unconscious little animal. From that time I began to have a soul."

Maud had her own brush with death when she was about five. She was visiting with her father's parents, the Montgomerys, who lived a few miles from the Macneill farm. One evening, Maud was watching the cook stir the hot coals in the fireplace with a long poker as they prepared dinner together. Maud liked to see the red-hot embers burn and fall apart. So she picked up the poker when the cook put it down—but she picked it up by the wrong end, the hot end. Maud burned her hand badly. After it was treated, she was sent to bed.

The following morning, Maud woke up complaining of a headache. Everyone thought she was sick because she was upset about burning her hand. But as the day wore on, the headache grew worse instead of better. Maud had a high fever, too. Finally, the doctor was called. He came to the house, examined Maud, and made a serious diagnosis: Maud had typhoid fever. Typhoid fever is an illness that affects the lungs and the intestines. Its symptoms include a rash and an extremely high temperature. A very bad case of it can be fatal.

Maud was sick in bed for many days. Her illness became so severe that Grandmother Macneill was sent for. Sometimes Maud recognized her grandmother. But at other times she was confused and delirious from the fever. Then, she insisted that her grandmother was old Mrs. Murphy, who worked around the house.

At last Maud began to feel better—and hungry. Doctors did not know then that it can be very dangerous for a person just recovering from typhoid to eat too much. So no one warned the Montgomerys to be careful as Maud's appetite returned to normal. One day Maud smelled sausages frying in the kitchen. That was what she wanted for her first meal after her illness: sausages, and *lots* of sausages. She did not get sick from her huge meal—and she was fortunate. Doctors now know that a meal like that so soon after typhoid could actually have killed her.

By the time Maud was three years old, she was learning to read. When she wasn't at home with a book she was off exploring the woods or the orchard or the beach that was only a half mile away: a little girl with long, light-brown hair who knew how to wiggle her ears.

Reading and stories fascinated Maud. One day, Grandmother Macneill was reading the newspaper aloud. One story in the paper said that a certain preacher was predicting that the world would end that very week—that Sunday, to be exact. As far as Maud was concerned, everything printed in the newspaper was a fact. She went through the days watching the sky for some omen or sign of the coming catastrophe. When Saturday arrived, Maud asked her aunt Emily if there would be Sunday school the next day. "Of course!" Aunt Emily answered, which helped Maud feel a little more confident that life would go on as usual. At last the dreaded day passed with the world still intact. Maud was relieved—and she had learned not to believe everything she read. In a way, she had discovered fiction.

One of her father's stories taught her about fiction, too, and about the difference between fiction and a lie.

On Grandfather Montgomery's mantelpiece there sat two dogs made of china, white with green spots. Maud loved the little dogs, and a story her father told about them whenever he visited. Maud's father said that every night, when they heard the clock chime midnight, those china dogs jumped down from the mantelpiece and barked. But Maud was never allowed to stay awake to see this wonderful sight. She finally told her father she didn't believe his story, that dogs made of china couldn't come to life. Maud's father insisted that they would—but they had to *hear* the clock chime. And dogs made of china can't hear.

Sometimes Maud played with her cousins, the Campbells, at Park Corner when she visited there. But because her grandparents were strict and didn't approve of fun and frivolity, she didn't have many other children to play with. So Maud invented imaginary playmates. In the house was a cabinet with two glass doors. Behind each glass door, Maud said, there lived a person, and she spent hours carrying on conversations with them. She especially liked to talk to the people in the cabinet at twilight, when the light from the fireplace threw reflections of sparkles and shadows onto the glass doors. In the right-hand door lived Katie Maurice, a girl Maud's own age. In the left-hand side of the cabinet lived a widow named Lucy Gray, an unhappy old woman who nevertheless told wonderful stories. Katie Maurice and Lucy Gray, through mutual dislike, did not speak to each other, only to Maud. Maud herself preferred Katie Maurice as a friend, because she was younger and more fun. But she was also careful not to neglect old Lucy Gray and her stories.

Soon, Maud gained two real friends. The Macneills' home was not far from the Cavendish schoolhouse. In those days, when there were no school buses, children who lived too far away to walk to school had two options. They could ride to school and back with someone who had a horse and carriage and who traveled in that direction, or they could board with a family that lived nearby. Because they lived in a good-sized house close by the school, the Macneills took in two young boarders, orphan boys named David and Wellington (or Well) Nelson. Maud had playmates at last! Maud was just a

Maud's childhood companions were Well and Dave Nelson, shown here with their sister.

week older than Well, the more studious of the two boys. Dave, who preferred to work with his hands, was a year younger. Both boys had tempers and loved to fight and wrestle just for the fun of it.

The three children played together around the Macneill farm. In the orchard they built a playhouse made of wooden posts and evergreen branches. They tried to plant a vegetable garden one summer, unsuccessfully. Only the sunflowers and the plants they neglected grew and thrived. Living so close to the ocean, the children spent countless hours at the beach. Despite her love of the ocean, Maud never learned to swim well. But she could wade and splash and wander on

The Macneill farmhouse in Cavendish, Prince Edward Island.

the shore. On those long walks by the water, the children feasted on dulse, a kind of edible seaweed that is still a popular snack on Prince Edward Island. Well and Dave even included Maud in their fishing expeditions. They were impressed by a girl who baited her own fishhooks and caught trout larger than theirs.

All three children—especially Maud—had vivid imaginations and liked to make up stories, especially ghost stories to frighten one another. Even many years later, Maud would write: "I like nothing better than a well-told ghost story, warranted to send a cold creep down your spine."

Many of the ghost stories Maud, Well, and Dave told took place in a little wooded area near the Macneill home, a place the children called the Haunted Wood. In their imaginations, ghosts and ghouls and fearful animals of fire inhabited the wood after dark, eager to chase unsuspecting wanderers. But most abundant of all were the nameless, shapeless "white things" that stalked among the trees. The "white things" could venture beyond the Haunted Wood, too—even to the gardens and orchard of the Macneill property.

One afternoon the three children were playing in the orchard. It was daylight, but that did not deter "white things." Suddenly the children caught sight of something large and white beneath a tree. At first they thought it was the homeless woman who wandered around Cavendish, or maybe a white calf. But while they stared, the thing began to creep along the ground toward them. The three children did not stop running or screaming about the "white thing" until they reached home. They told their story so convincingly that several household workers grabbed pitchforks and buckets and headed toward the orchard to investigate. But they found nothing unsual. Soon afterward Grandmother Macneill came home to a house full of hysterical stories of ghosts. As it happened, Grandmother Macneill *had* seen the "white thing." That day she had washed a big white tablecloth and set it out in the sun to dry. In fact, she had just returned from fetching it out of the orchard.

A quarter century later, in the old Macneill farmhouse, Maud would sit down to begin writing a book. The Haunted Wood would find a place in that book. So would Lucy Gray and Katie Maurice in their cabinethome, and the nearby sea, and Prince Edward Island's brilliant green fields and peculiar red-dirt roads. "Were it not for those Cavendish years," Maud once said, "I do not think *Anne of Green Gables* would ever have been written."

Chapter 2

 aud Montgomery had an auspicious heritage for a future writer. She came from a long line of storytellers and poets. In her heritage was also a spark of spirit and gumption, especially on the female side. Gumption was something a girl who wanted to be a writer needed plenty of around the turn of the century. Most successful writers of the day were men. While there were a number of female authors, too, many found it necessary to use masculine pen names to gain greater respect for their work.

Maud's family roots on her mother's side were mainly in England; on her father's side, in Scotland. Her family could trace its history all the way back to the Norman Conquest of England in 1066. There were even people with titles in the family. Since 1508, the Earl of Eglinton had been a Montgomery. The family had its share of writers, too. A Macneill in Scotland, an ancestor of Maud's mother, had been a talented, recognized poet, as had a member of her father's family.

Both the Macneills and the Montgomerys arrived on Prince Edward Island in the mid-1700s. The Montgomerys were proud of many firsts in their family. A Montgomery was the first English-speaking settler in Malpeque, a town near Cavendish. That was in 1769. Donald Montgomery, Maud's grandfather, was appointed to the Canadian Senate. He was one of the first men to represent Prince Edward Island in the national government.

Maud grew up hearing stories about her family's history. One of those stories was about Hugh Montgomery, Maud's great-great-great-grandfather—the first Montgomery to come to the New World. When Hugh Montgomery set out from England to Canada, he was planning to settle on the mainland. But his wife, Mary MacShannon Montgomery, was very seasick throughout the long Atlantic crossing. When the boat landed at Prince Edward Island, Mary Montgomery went ashore. After finally setting foot on dry, solid land again, she firmly refused to step onto another boat. Thanks to her, the Montgomery family was established on Prince Edward Island.

Then there was the story of another Donald Montgomery, Maud's great-grandfather. Donald wanted to marry Nancy Penman, one of the most beautiful girls the Island had ever seen. Of course, Nancy had many other suitors, especially a young man named David

Murray. Finally, to get Nancy's attention, Donald hitched a steer to a wood-sled and drove the strange contraption to the Penmans' doorstep. David Murray was disappointed about losing Nancy—but not for long. Nancy Penman had an equally beautiful, strong-willed sister named Betsy, who lost no time proposing to Nancy's attractive, jilted suitor. Donald and Nancy's son married David and Betsy's daughter—so both of the beautiful, independent Penman sisters were Maud's great-grandmothers.

Cousins were always marrying cousins in the little town of Cavendish. There were three main families in the town: the Simpsons, the Macneills, and the Clarks, all fiercely proud of their status in the community. It was a rare person in Cavendish who wasn't related to one—and often to two—of the families.

The finest storyteller by far in Maud's family was Aunt Mary Lawson. She was old when Maud was a young girl, but the two got along well. Aunt Mary Lawson held her niece entranced with her tales of old family romances. "She was really quite the most wonderful woman in many respects that I have ever known," Maud recalled.

Besides the stories Maud heard, stories that shaped her future as a writer, there were also the stories she read. Her family placed a high value on books and reading. From a very early age, Maud was exposed to the finest authors: Shakespeare, Sir Walter Scott, and the great British and American poets. Although they had only average educations, both her Macneill and Montgomery grandparents kept excellent libraries in their homes.

In a family as strict and religious as the Macneills were, Maud was exposed to literature of another kind. On Sundays, no one in the household was allowed to do any work. The family was not even permitted to read, unless it was a religious or inspirational book. The adults read the Bible or pages from a collection of sermons. Maud preferred a book called *The Memoir of Anzonetta Peters*. Anzonetta Peters was a ten-year-old fictional girl who was too perfect and too good to be true. She endured all sorts of difficulties and never complained. After a long and painful illness, which she also suffered through without complaining, she died a saintly death, speaking the words of a hymn. Besides all this, Anzonetta Peters did not carry on ordinary conversations. Everything she said was quoted from the Bible.

Anzonetta Peters fascinated Maud. She thought about "talking Scripture," but decided that people would laugh at her if she did. So, in her journals, she tried *writing* "in Scripture" like Anzonetta Peters. Maud soon got tired of that, too. Somebody saintly like Anzonetta Peters might be an interesting character for a book, Maud decided, but it was much more fun to be a real, rebellious, often-in-trouble girl.

Maud attended the Cavendish school near her grandparents' home—the same school Well and Dave Nelson attended. It was a one-room schoolhouse, where small children and teenagers were taught by the same teacher. When she started going to school, Maud was already able to read. She was precocious, curious, and creative, and would have been a model student except for her stubbornness and independence. One of her

Maud attended the one-room schoolhouse in Cavendish.

teachers would not allow his students to use slang expressions. Maud would never forget the whipping he gave her for saying "by the skin of our teeth," which he claimed was slang. Very self-righteously, Maud continued to assert that the phrase was not slang, but was from the Bible. She was right: It is in the Book of Job.

At school, Maud often felt that she didn't fit in. For instance, she dressed differently, since her grandmother made her clothes. One year the pattern for Maud's dresses was exceptionally ugly. The other girls laughed and called her outfits "baby aprons." Maud kept hoping that the aprons would wear out so she could get new dresses, but, unfortunately, the sturdy material lasted and lasted. Some girls might have laughed at her

clothes, but others envied Maud's leather, buttoned
shoes, while she wished she would be allowed to go to
school barefoot and comfortable on warm days.

Most of the children brought their lunches to school
with them because they lived too far from the school
to go home at noon. They set their little bottles of milk
in a stream to stay cool until lunchtime. Then they ate
outdoors in a pleasant grove of trees. But because she
lived so near, Maud went home for lunch.

Her grandfather, who ran the Cavendish post office,
sometimes brought home sheets of a kind of scrap paper
used to print post office bills. On these letter-bills,
Maud began her writing career.

Maud especially loved poetry. When she was nine
years old, she decided to try writing a poem herself.
She had grown up reading the works of the great British
and American poets, and she wrote her first poem,
"Autumn," in blank verse to imitate their style. Blank
verse has a definite rhythm, but it does not rhyme.
Maud's poem began:

> Now autumn comes, laden with peach and pear;
> The sportsman's horn is heard throughout the land,
> And the poor partridge, fluttering, falls dead.

Maud's father happened to be home on a visit when
she wrote "Autumn." She was proud of her accomplishment, and of course showed it to him. "What kind
of poetry is this?" Mr. Montgomery asked when he
noticed that it didn't rhyme.

"Blank verse," Maud answered.

"Very blank," was Mr. Montgomery's verdict. From

By the time Maud was ten, she knew she wanted to be a writer.

then on, Maud tried very hard to make her poetry rhyme. Many years later, a friend and fellow writer asked Maud which came first when she wrote poetry, the idea or the rhyme. Maud replied that she first wrote down her ideas, setting them into some sort of rhythm, but without a thought to rhyme. That came next, often with the help of a rhyming dictionary.

Maud had a friend and classmate named Alma who

also liked to write poetry. At first the two girls wrote
about nature and seasons and general things. But they
soon discovered that it was more fun to write little
verses about their classmates and teachers. Sometimes,
when they were supposed to be doing their lessons in
class, the girls wrote poems instead. They secretly
passed the poems back and forth, both girls trying hard
not to laugh at the latest descriptions.

In the late 1800s, schoolchildren did not do their
classroom assignments on paper. They wrote on slates,
which were little desk-size blackboards. Slates were
quick and easy to erase—which made them ideal for
passing notes!

One day, Maud and Alma were busy passing poems
to each other on their slates. Their teacher suspected
that it was not his lesson the two girls found so amusing.
He saw the slate being passed, and he intercepted it.
Before Maud could erase the poem—about that very
teacher—from her slate, he had it in his hand. Maud
was terrified that he would read the poem aloud, in
front of the whole class. But he didn't even look at
what was written. Maud always believed it was because
he knew it was something about himself, something he
really didn't want to know. Instead, the teacher handed
the slate back to Maud without a word. That was the
last time Maud and Alma passed poems about teachers
in class. Years later, in one of her novels, Maud wrote
about a girl named Emily who suffered through a similar embarrassing situation—except Emily's poem *was*
read aloud.

Maud liked her poems, and so did the friends she

shared them with. All she needed was a little encouragement to try to share them with an even larger audience.

She saw her opportunity when a teacher named Izzie Robinson was boarding at her grandfather's house. Miss Robinson considered herself a talented singer. Gathering all her courage, Maud asked the woman whether she knew a song called "Evening Dreams."

Miss Robinson wasn't familiar with the title, so she asked Maud to recite the words. But there was no way Izzie Robinson could have known "Evening Dreams." Maud herself had written the poem.

> When the evening sun is setting
> Quietly in the west
> In a halo of rainbow glory
> I sit me down to rest
>
> I forget the present and the future,
> I live over the past once more
> As I see before me crowding
> The beautiful days of yore.

Miss Robinson listened as Maud recited. She finally said that she didn't know the song; but the words, she added, were "very pretty."

That was all the encouragement Maud needed. She decided that her poem was ready for publication. Maud did not know that anything submitted for publication should be typed. She did not know that, if she wanted her poem returned, she had to enclose postage and an envelope. She simply copied "Evening Dreams" onto a clean sheet of paper, in her best handwriting, and sent it off to an American magazine. She didn't tell anyone about it. And she certainly wasn't hoping for payment—she didn't even know "that people were ever paid for writing." A few weeks later, "Evening Dreams" came back in the mail, rejected.

Undaunted, Maud tried again. This time, she sent the poem to a local newspaper that often published poems by writers from the area. Maud was sure that "Evening Dreams" was just as good as anything the paper accepted and printed. But once again, the poem came back with a rejection note.

This time Maud *was* discouraged. It would be years before she had enough confidence in her work to try again.

But this didn't stop her from writing just for the sheer joy of it. Now she was also writing stories. At school, she became the center of a group of girls who liked to write, too. Maud and her friends Amanda and Janie formed a story club. They each wrote a story about a young woman who drowned tragically at the Cavendish beach just to see how similar or different their ideas would be. All the stories came out sad and romantic, and naturally, Maud's was judged the best. Of the three girls, only Maud wanted to continue writing fiction.

Tragedy was Maud's specialty. She wrote one long, sad story called "My Graves," about the wife of a traveling Methodist minister. At each stop along his circuit, from Newfoundland to Vancouver, his wife has a baby, who always dies. So by the end of the story, the young woman has left an amazing string of infant graves across Canada.

Around the same time, Maud wrote "The History of Flossy Brighteyes," the biography of a doll. Flossy Brighteyes survives adventure after tragic adventure. "I couldn't kill a doll," Maud said later, "but I dragged her through every other tribulation." In Flossy Brighteyes's old age, she finally falls into the hands of a good and loving child, and the story has a happy ending.

By the time she was fifteen and nearing the end of what we would now call junior high school, Maud had won some awards for her writing. The most prestigious was third place in the county for the Canada Prize, sponsored by a newspaper, the *Montreal Witness*. The prize was for an essay about an event in Canadian history. Maud chose to write about an event she had witnessed when she was eight years old: the shipwreck of the *Marco Polo*.

The *Marco Polo* was a clipper ship, a large ocean-going sailing vessel used especially for carrying cargo in the 1800s. Clipper ships were built for speed, and when she was new, the *Marco Polo* was the fastest ship in the world.

But long years of traveling on the rough seas had, by 1883, taken their toll. The *Marco Polo* had become a rather dangerous, decrepit old hulk. She sailed out of Quebec in late July with a cargo of lumber. On Wednesday, July 25, just off Prince Edward Island, the *Marco Polo* ran into a terrible storm. The crew lost control of the vessel. All they could do was let the wild winds blow her where they would and hope that somehow they could reach land safely. The crippled ship careened straight toward the Cavendish beach.

"The vessel, coming before the gale, with every stitch of canvas set, was a sight never to be forgotten," Maud recalled. While many of the residents of Cavendish watched in fascination and horror, the *Marco Polo* finally ran aground just three hundred yards off the Cavendish shore.

Luckily, the crew were all safe. They spent the next several weeks boarding with the people of Cavendish. It was an exotic time for the quiet little town, with a ruined, 1,625-ton clipper ship swaying just off its shore and twenty colorful sailors of many nationalities, languages, and races staying in its homes. Maud would never forget the day the captain, who was boarding with the Macneills, gathered the crew to distribute their pay. The Macneills' parlor table was covered to overflowing with gold coins.

The *Marco Polo* itself could not be made seaworthy again. But its cargo was still on board, and many things on the ship were valuable. So, on an evening when the weather appeared calm and fair, some members of the salvage crew set out for the wreck. They decided to spend the night on the ruined ship. While they were aboard the *Marco Polo*, another storm suddenly blew up in the night. The men struggled to reach the shore in the fierce waves, while local fishermen watched, helpless to assist them without endangering their own lives. This time they were not as fortunate: One local man who had been helping with the salvage was drowned.

An auction was held in Cavendish to sell the rigging and cargo of the *Marco Polo*. This attracted many more colorful and exotic characters. Maud was right there

at the auction, notebook in hand, observing everything. She also sampled a "delicacy" well known to the
sailors: hardtack, a tough biscuit that never seemed to
go stale. The local children nearly broke their teeth
trying to chew the hardtack that was spread out on the
Marco Polo's sail—but once it was moistened a little,
it was sweet and delicious.

From her notes and her marvelous memory, seven
years later Maud was able to reconstruct the stormy
Wednesday morning of the shipwreck to write her
prize-winning essay.

Two essays ranked higher than Maud's in the county
competition. Ironically, one of these essays was by
Maud's school sweetheart, Nate Lockhart. There was
a school superstition: "If you count nine stars for nine
continuous nights the first boy you shake hands with
afterward is to be your future husband." Always a
romantic at heart, Maud counted the stars—and shook
hands with Nate. He was a good writer, and one of his
uncles was a poet. Perhaps, if things had been different, Nate and Maud would have made a likely match.

When Maud was nine years old, she had kept a diary,
which she kept hidden on a shelf under the sitting room
sofa. But she hadn't had much that was exciting to
write in the diary—mainly, she recorded the
weather—so after a while she lost interest in it.

Then, on September 21, 1889, she had written on
the first page of a new notebook: "Life is beginning to
get interesting for me." That was part of the first entry
in a journal she would keep faithfully for the next fifty-
three years.

And life *was* beginning to get interesting for Maud. In the following year, her *Marco Polo* essay would win her recognition. She would part from all the school friends she had known since childhood.

And she would travel nearly across the continent to rejoin her father—and meet her new family.

ugh John Montgomery was one of the many
people who migrated to Canada's western provinces as
those vast lands opened up. Sometimes he worked for
the government, but always he worked for himself, too.
Officially, for a while, he was employed by an organization that recruited and settled people in the prairie
province of Saskatchewan. On and off, Mr. Montgomery was also a real estate agent, an auctioneer, a broker,
and an issuer of patents for inventions. In 1884 he was
hired by the Canadian government as a forest ranger.
But he still continued his outside jobs. After a while
he lost his government post, but by that time his self-
made jobs were sufficient to support him—and, before
long, a new family.

In April of 1887, ten years after Clara Woolner Macneill Montgomery's death, Hugh John Montgomery re-married. His new wife was Mary Ann MacRae, the daughter of his boss. Soon the couple had a baby, a little girl they named Kate. Maud had a half-sister.

With his new family, Hugh John Montgomery settled

In 1887 Hugh John Montgomery married Mary Ann MacRae. They soon invited Maud to join them in Saskatchewan.

in Prince Albert, Saskatchewan, a growing, prosperous prairie town.

Like his daughter Maud, Hugh John Montgomery also liked to name things. He called his house in Prince Albert Eglintoune Villa because, back in Great Britain, the Montgomerys' ancestors had been the earls of an estate called Eglinton. Proud of his heritage, Hugh John Montgomery founded a society for people of Scottish ancestry in Prince Albert.

Now that he was settled down in a real home in a relatively comfortable frontier town, Mr. Montgomery decided that he had been separated from his oldest daughter long enough. He had never felt right about leaving her to be raised by her grandparents, and Maud missed him during the long months and years between his visits. To reunite her family was one of her fondest dreams. In the early summer of 1890, Mr. Montgomery sent a letter to Maud, inviting her to join him, his new wife, and baby Kate in Prince Albert, Saskatchewan.

At the beginning of that summer of 1890, Maud said good-bye to her school friends. Some she knew she would never see again, especially now that she was moving away. Many of the young people exchanged "ten-year letters." The person who received a ten-year letter promised not to open or read it until ten years later—it was a sort of personal time capsule. One of Maud's ten-year letters was from Nate Lockhart, the first boy ever to tell her that he loved her.

By the end of that summer, Maud was also preparing to leave her beloved Prince Edward Island for the first time in her life. She would be traveling to Saskatchewan with Grandfather Montgomery. He was also eager to

The trip across Canada was exciting for teenage Maud, who had never been off Prince Edward Island.

visit his son and meet his new daughter-in-law and grandchild. In August, laden with trunks full of clothing and personal belongings, Maud and her grandfather took a ferry to the mainland. Once there, they boarded a train. For Maud, that was another first.

Maud's companion on her trip to Saskatchewan was her grandfather on her father's side, "Senator" Montgomery.

The train sped across the open Canadian prairie, climbing up to the western plateau. In her fifteen years on green, sea-swept Prince Edward Island, Maud had never seen anything like the prairie, with its flower-bedecked expanses of tall grass and occasional stands of spindly trees.

The railroad line to Prince Albert was not quite finished; it was due to be completed about three weeks after Maud and Grandfather Montgomery reached Saskatchewan. So the travelers had to leave the train in the town of Regina. They arrived at their hotel—and, to their surprise, there to meet them was Hugh John Montgomery! It was a joyful reunion, for Maud and her grandfather had not seen him for five years. The Montgomery family then set out on the rough journey from Regina to Prince Albert.

On Friday, August 22, 1890, Maud, her father, and her grandfather rode into the town of Prince Albert, and Maud met her stepmother, Mary Ann MacRae Montgomery. Very quickly, it became clear that it would not be a friendly relationship.

Maud was fifteen years old the summer she traveled to Saskatchewan. Her stepmother was twenty-seven, only twelve years older. Being so very close in age, it was difficult for them to think of themselves as mother and daughter. But Mary Ann Montgomery wanted to assert herself in her new role. For Mrs. Montgomery, this meant that she would make the rules, and Maud would be expected to obey them. She immediately began assigning Maud chores to do. She was pregnant, so Maud's chores steadily increased. Maud started to feel more like a servant than a stepdaughter. While for his sake she was never openly disrespectful to her father's new wife, Maud felt no great affection toward her either. She finally took to addressing her as "Mrs.

The Montgomery home in Prince Albert, Saskatchewan, was called Eglintoune Villa.

Montgomery," unless her father insisted on something more familiar when company was present.

Prince Albert was comfortable as frontier towns went, with shops and a hotel and churches. But it had grown up quickly and without much planning, and in some ways, its slapdash quality showed. The original settlers had been men, working in lumbering or mining or building. At first these men had not brought families with them. But as the town grew, families arrived, including children. Children needed schools, so old buildings—or parts of them—were converted into classrooms.

The high school in Prince Albert was in the same building as a hotel. Upstairs from the classrooms was the ballroom. Whenever there was a dance, the classrooms were used as ladies' dressing rooms. Occasionally Maud and her classmates would discover feathers or flowers or hairpins, or even hand mirrors, in the classroom afterward. The police station and the jail were also in the same building. The cells backed onto the schoolrooms. Sometimes the students on their way to class would pass the day's catch of criminals on their way to the cells. Once, Maud let her curiosity get the better of her. When no one was around, she went exploring in the jail. She'd just let herself into one of the cells when the door slammed shut behind her—and locked! She was a prisoner in the Prince Albert jail for several anxious hours.

In her school on Prince Edward Island, Maud had enjoyed some outstandingly enthusiastic and creative teachers. She found the quality of education in Prince Albert uninspired and uninspiring. Mr. Mustard, the high school's headmaster, was a bachelor, a shy, plain man who wanted to be a minister, not a schoolteacher. Maud's stepmother began to invite him to visit in the evening. Then she would go out herself or find some chore that needed doing, leaving Maud to try to entertain Mr. Mustard. Though he was quite a bit older than Maud, it soon became clear that Mrs. Montgomery was hoping a romance would develop between her independent stepdaughter and the stodgy schoolteacher. Eventually, he actually started talking about marriage to Maud. She had never been impressed by Mr. Mustard as a teacher; she was even less impressed by him as a prospective husband—and she tried to tell him this as gently, but as firmly, as she could. In a letter to one of her cousins back on Prince Edward Island,

Maud wrote: "I heartily wish Mr. Mustard and his High School were in Venezuela."

Because of all the work she had to do at home, Maud missed a lot of school. In February 1891, Mrs. Montgomery had her baby, a boy named Bruce. There was now more work than ever. Maud stopped going to school altogether. But she continued to read and to write whenever she could find the time, and her writing was gaining recognition.

During the fall of 1890, Maud was working on a poem about an old story popular on Prince Edward Island: the legend of Cape LeForce. According to this tale, back in pirate days, when Prince Edward Island belonged to France and was called Ile St.-Jean, a pirate ship anchored off Cape LeForce on the island. The crew went ashore for the night with the rich loot of a recent raid. There arose an argument between the pirate ship's captain and the first mate. They decided to settle the argument with a duel. The two men took their weapons and turned to walk the designated number of paces, for duels were very formal affairs, with strict rules. Suddenly, before reaching his spot, the first mate spun around and fired his pistol. The captain fell dead on the shore. He was buried there on the rocky cape. Maud's grandfather claimed to have seen the grave when he'd been young, before the waves eroded it into the sea.

Maud retold "The Legend of Cape LeForce" in the form of a poem. Unknown to her friends or her family, she sent a copy to a newspaper in Prince Edward Island's capital city, the *Charlottetown Patriot*. It was three years since Maud had tried to publish the poem "Evening Dreams." That rejection had hurt—but Maud had a lot of confidence in "The Legend of Cape LeForce."

On Sunday, December 7, Mr. Montgomery came to the breakfast table with the mail from the day before. One of the items was a *Charlottetown Patriot* dated November 26, and in the paper was Maud's poem! Despite a few words the paper had misspelled, Maud could say: "This has really been the proudest day of my life! I feel at least three inches taller than I did yesterday."

Her poem's success encouraged Maud to try publishing more of her writing. The Saskatchewan prairie was very different from the maritime town where Maud had spent the first fifteen years of her life. It was even different from what she had read about the West. The thunderstorms were more violent than any she'd experienced in the East. The vistas were more rugged. And the Native Americans she saw were nothing like the characters in James Fenimore Cooper's adventure novels. The western Indians Maud met were poor, struggling to make livings as farmers or herdsmen or cowboys or craftsmen, totally unlike Cooper's noble savages in handmade buckskin and feathers. In some ways, Maud was disappointed that the real West did not match its reputation or her expectations. But she could not help being fascinated by it.

Maud wrote an essay entitled "A Western Eden," about her perspectives on her new home. In June of 1891 it was printed in the *Prince Albert Times*. Other newspapers in the Canadian West noticed the article, liked it, and reprinted it.

Around the same time, Maud sent a short story to the *Montreal Witness*, and it won a prize. So far she had received no money as payment for her writing; but for now, though she knew that some writers were paid for their work, she was satisfied simply with seeing her poem, story, or essay in print, with her name below the title.

Maud was becoming successful with her writing, and she had many friends in her new home. In the winter, the young people of Prince Albert went tobogganing and sleighing; in the summer, they enjoyed picnics and berry picking. Maud was involved in all sorts of clubs and societies, and was teaching a church Sunday school class. Anne Shirley, Maud's most famous character, would one day call her special friends "kindred spirits." When Maud met Will and Laura Pritchard in Prince Albert, she found her "kindred spirits." Maud gave Will Pritchard a ring. It was not an engagement ring, but it was very special to them both. Will died when he was young, in his twenties. Afterward, his sister Laura returned the ring to Maud, and Maud continued to wear it until the day she died.

In spite of her friends and activities, Maud was unhappy. Her stepmother was increasingly demanding with two small children to care for, and she was jealous of Maud's close relationship with her father. Mr. Montgomery, who was getting involved in politics, did not seem to notice that his "Maudie" was being treated like a servant.

On New Year's Day 1891, Maud's deepest wish had been to go home. She loved her father and always would. She had tried to like his new family. But they would not change, and neither could Maud. On a summer day in 1891, Maud's New Year's wish came true. Sixteen years old, about to cross a continent alone, she boarded a train to return to Prince Edward Island.

o that autumn, Maud was back home in Cavendish, on the island she loved. But she was not sure what she wanted to do with herself. In the late 1800s, there was little pressure for girls to finish high school, and even less to go on to college, unless they wanted to be teachers. Girls generally did not get an education just for the sake of getting an education. Often they married very young, as young as sixteen, and spent the rest of their lives managing the household and raising a family.

Maud knew how valuable a good education was for a writer, but her grandparents were not very supportive of her dream. They wondered why the ordinary life of a Cavendish housewife wasn't good enough for their granddaughter.

So, for a while, Maud gave music lessons to local children. She was able to play the piano and the organ quite well. Sometimes she also played the organ in her church. In the meantime, she wrote as much as she could. And she continued to send her stories and poems to a variety of magazines—any magazine she thought might be interested in her work. She had no illusions that she was writing great literature. She knew that she could be a far more skillful writer if she had more time and more training.

After about a year of giving music lessons and writing, and dreaming of all the wonderful things she could be doing with her life, Maud made a decision. She was going back to school. She wanted to be a teacher.

Prince of Wales College in Charlottetown, the capital of Prince Edward Island, offered courses leading to a teacher's license. But to get into the program, the prospective student had to pass a rigorous examination. Maud had been out of school for a long time, and she hadn't learned much at the high school in Prince Albert. So she returned to her old school in Cavendish to study for the college entrance examination.

Two hundred sixty-four students took the examination at the same time Maud did. Her score was the fifth highest.

Maud's grandparents finally relented and agreed to finance her tuition at Prince of Wales College. She moved into a spare room in the home of Mrs. Alexander MacMillan, a widow in Charlottetown. Besides Maud and her landlady, Mrs. MacMillan's three children (a daughter and two sons) and another boarder also lived in the house. Boarders not only lived in their landlord or landlady's home, they also ate meals with the family; and Maud, who liked good food, was never happy with the quality of Mrs. MacMillan's cooking. But, since boarding with the Macmillans was both convenient and economical, Maud stayed with them.

Maud hardly had time to settle into her room before she began attending classes at Prince of Wales College. She had decided to try to complete the equivalent of two years of courses in one year to save money, so she was very busy with schoolwork. Nevertheless, she found time to be on the staff of the school's literary magazine.

Sometimes school was even fun. One day, all the students in Maud's chemistry class conspired to throw a "peanut party." Suddenly, in the middle of class, the students began to pull out sacks of roasted peanuts, eating them and throwing the empty shells across the room at each other. The teacher was powerless in the midst of the classwide food fight.

At the end of the school year, Maud had to take two sets of exams. One set determined her grades in the courses she had taken. The other set was required for all prospective teachers. Both were very difficult. And there were only a few days to rest between the two exhausting sessions of tests. Maud worried about her grades—but she had little to worry about. She earned the highest score in her class in English drama, literature, agriculture, and school management. Each year, the best English essay was presented at graduation. That year, the essay was Maud's.

When her term at Prince of Wales College was over, Maud returned to her grandparents' home in Cavendish. Now that she had a teacher's license, the next step was to find a job as a teacher. Today, most people apply for a job by first writing a letter. Then, people generally applied for jobs, including teaching jobs, in person. Maud began to hear about schools that needed teachers. She asked her grandfather to drive her in his horse and carriage to those schools so she could apply for the jobs. Grandfather Macneill refused. Maud's grandparents simply would not support her goals of getting a good education and finding a job. They believed that what she needed to learn and do, she could learn and do at home. Maud also suspected that Grandfather Macneill disliked teachers because he'd once had a bad experience with a teacher who boarded with the family. If Maud wanted a teaching job, she would have to find a way to get it herself. So she sent out letter after letter, applying for positions in schools all around Prince Edward Island. If a school accepted her, it would have to do so without meeting her in person— and she would be accepting the job without seeing the school.

Finally, the school in the town of Bideford offered Maud a job. She was disappointed when she arrived there. It was a one-room schoolhouse, like the school Maud herself had attended in Cavendish, but the little building was bare and isolated on a dull hilltop.

On her first day as a teacher at Bideford, Maud had twenty students of all ages and grade levels in her classroom. That night Maud wrote in her journal: "I had a rather hard time all day."

If her first day was hard with twenty students, the following days grew even harder. Each morning, another youngster or two arrived at Maud's school. Before long, forty-eight students were crowded into the single classroom. Some were bright and motivated and eager to learn, as Maud had been as a child. Most weren't. Day by day, Maud came to appreciate the toils of all the teachers she'd had, and she saw how much she had to learn.

While she was working in Bideford, Maud boarded with the Reverend Estey, a Methodist minister, and his wife. Maud lived with the Esteys and their little daugh-

While she taught school in Bideford, Maud lived at the manse with the Reverend Estey and his family.

ter (one of Maud's students) in the manse, the house the church provided for the minister. One day, Mrs. Estey was entertaining some guests, one of whom was another minister. Mrs. Estey wanted to fix a special cake for the occasion, but in her hurry, she grabbed the wrong bottle when she added the flavoring. It wasn't until the guests began eating the cake that she realized the mistake she'd made. Instead of flavoring, she'd grabbed a bottle of anodyne liniment—a kind of medication used to soothe sprains and aching muscles. The other guests ate one bite of the cake and refused any more. But the visiting minister graciously ate the entire piece and never said a word about the peculiar taste. Maud would later use this embarrassing incident in *Anne of Green Gables*. All the interesting things that happened around a person like Maud were liable to end up in some form in her writing.

For despite all the work she had preparing and teaching her classes, Maud continued to write. Under the pen name Maud Cavendish, her writing was becoming quite successful. Women's magazines in Canada and the United States accepted her poems. There was no money involved, only the "honor," Maud noted, of being published. Then a short story was accepted. "No pay yet—but that may come some day," said Maud hopefully. Two free subscriptions to a magazine were the closest Maud had come to getting paid so far.

By the end of the school year, Maud had earned $179.58 teaching at Bideford, a low salary even for that time. But, except for the cost of her room and board with the Esteys, she had been able to save most of the money she earned. It was almost enough to pay for one year at a real college.

Maud decided to take a year off from teaching. She thought that perhaps, if she were more familiar with famous writers and their books, she could improve her own writing. She was especially interested in a literature course being offered by a teacher and poet named Archibald Mechan at Dalhousie College in Halifax, Nova Scotia. Grandmother Macneill, seeing her granddaughter's determination, agreed to give Maud the extra money she needed to enroll in Dalhousie.

Dalhousie was a coeducational college: Young women could take courses alongside the young men. But there were no women's dormitories. Female students had to board elsewhere. A half mile away was Halifax Ladies' College; many of the girls enrolled in courses at Dalhousie took rooms there. Maud, too, decided to live at Ladies' College. At first she shared a room with another girl. But after a while a single room on the top floor of the dormitory building opened up, and Maud hurried to take it. To earn a little extra money, Maud offered music lessons.

Maud's year at Dalhousie College was an eventful one. First, a girl at Ladies' College caught the measles. When Maud began to feel headachy and sick, too, she thought it was just a bad cold, for she'd had a succession of colds since coming to Halifax. But soon her eyes started hurting, and she broke out in a rash. Maud also had the measles. She was put into a quarantined room where no one could visit. Her only companion was the other girl with the measles—and she was not someone whose company Maud especially liked. Because of her illness, Maud missed quite a few classes. Nevertheless, she passed her courses with high marks.

While she was at Dalhousie, Maud was finally paid for something she had written. In fact, in one week she suddenly got checks from three different publishers!

On Monday of that exciting week, Maud found a five-dollar check in the mail. She had sent a short story to a children's magazine, called *Golden Days*, in Philadelphia. They had not only accepted the story, they had paid for it!

Another five dollars arrived on Wednesday. This time the money was from a newspaper in Halifax, the *Evening Mail*. The paper had sponsored a contest looking for a letter with the best aswer to the question: Who is more patient, men or women? Maud had entered the contest with a witty little poem. Instead of signing her real name, she used the pen name Belinda Bluegrass. Her poem had won first prize.

Finally, on Saturday, there came a check for twelve dollars from a magazine called *Youth's Companion*, which had accepted one of Maud's poems. Maud was especially excited about this last sale, and not only because the check was the largest. *Youth's Companion* had an excellent reputation and accepted only work of the highest quality.

Maud took her earnings to a bookshop and bought five volumes of poems by some of her favorite poets: Tennyson, Byron, Milton, Longfellow, and Whittier. While she was in town, she also had a professional photographer take her picture. That week, the word spread around the Dalhousie College campus that

Maud Montgomery not only wrote, but got paid for her writing.

Before long Maud was receiving more checks for poems and stories. The amounts were small—sometimes five dollars, sometimes less. Maud was excited with each successful publication, but writing while attending college was hard work, and only a small percentage of what Maud wrote was being accepted then. So she was also feeling frustrated. "People envy me these bits of success," she said, "and say, 'It's well to be you,' and so on. I smile cynically when I hear them. They do not realize how many disappointments come to one success. They see only the successes and think all must be smooth travelling."

For Maud, the traveling was far from smooth. She would have loved to stay at Dalhousie College and get her B.A., but she simply could not afford another term. Little, occasional checks for five or three dollars did not pay tuition. And Maud's grandparents would not do more to finance her ambitions. She was still very alone in her quest for an education and her dream of becoming a writer.

At the end of the semester, Maud returned to Prince Edward Island, and to teaching. Years later, looking back at her year at Dalhousie, Maud felt that it was a waste of time and money, something she would not do again if she had her life to live over. This was not because of the quality of the education. It was because the few courses Maud took were not as worthwhile as a real college degree.

Maud's next teaching job was in a town called Belmont. In some ways, Maud found Belmont very much like Bideford: another bare building, another bleak hill. The class was even less motivated.

Writing at Belmont was difficult, too. Maud boarded in a farmhouse during a winter that was particularly cold. The only time she could find to write was very early in the morning, before the family was up to light the fire and warm the house. At 6:00 A.M., Maud would sit indoors in her heaviest winter coat and boots, sometimes with gloves on her hands in the minus-twenty degrees Fahrenheit cold, to spend an hour at her writing.

Maud decided not to stay another year at Belmont. Once again, she found herself looking for a job. This time an opening arose in the town of Lower Bedeque.

For a while it seemed that this was the last job Maud would need. Maud's second cousin, Edwin Simpson, had begun courting her. When he proposed, Maud accepted.

But as the engagement wore on, Maud grew more and more uncertain that she wanted to marry Ed. He planned to become a minister, and Maud did not like the idea of being a minister's wife. Maud enjoyed music and dancing and fun—things ministers' wives then were not supposed to like. Also Maud and her cousin were of different religions. Ed was a Baptist, and Maud was a Presbyterian. That difference made her uncomfortable.

Worst of all, Maud began to realize that she *liked* Ed Simpson—but she didn't love him. Once, when he visited her, Maud ran to her room, locked the door, threw herself onto the floor, and muttered, "I can never

Maud was engaged for a while to her cousin Edwin Simpson.

marry him—*never*, NEVER, *NEVER*!" After that out-burst, she calmly went back downstairs and spent the evening talking with him—and keeping her distance from him. "I could not *bear* the mere touch of the man I had promised to marry," she said miserably.

Maud was unsure of what to do. She knew her cousin would provide her with a comfortable life and good companionship. But she also knew that she could not love him. So she allowed the engagement to drag on and on. And as much as possible, she tried to avoid seeing Ed.

While she taught in Lower Bedeque, Maud boarded with the Leard family. The Leards were poor farmers whose children had only the most basic education and saw no need for more. One of the Leard boys, Herman, was about Maud's age and quite handsome.

As the school year went by, Herman Leard and Maud began to go out of their way to see more of each other—and they fell passionately in love. Maud knew that she could not marry a man like Herman Leard. He was jealous of her writing and did not share or understand her ambitions. Maud liked a good intellectual argument, one that made you think; Herman was not interested in improving his mind. Nevertheless, Maud loved him desperately.

Once, Maud was caught in the uncomfortable situation of having Ed Simpson visit her at the Leards' home—while Herman was there. "There I was under the same roof with two men, one of whom I loved and could never marry, the other whom I had promised to marry but could never love!" Maud knew she could not remain engaged to Ed Simpson under the circumstances: Rumors about her and Herman Leard were spreading already. So she broke off the engagement in a letter. "It is an abominable business—this telling a man you can't marry him," she said.

Eventually, she had to give the same news to Herman Leard. Difficult as it was while they were living in the same house, Maud made it clear that the courtship was hopeless and pointless.

In the midst of all these emotional crises, something

happened that put Maud's personal life, including any thoughts of marriage, on hold for the next thirteen years. Grandfather Macneill died.

As quickly as she could, Maud quit her job in Lower Bedeque and returned to Cavendish. Grandmother Macneill would continue to live in the old house and run the post office, as her husband had. But she was getting old and needed help doing what had to be done. That help would have to come from her grand-daughter.

Maud was doing a lot of writing, sending her stories and poems to a longer and longer list of magazines. Some of what she wrote she managed to sell on the first attempt. But nine out of ten of her manuscripts came back rejected at least once. She was proud of her successes, but she preferred to keep her failures secret. Now that she was back working at the Cavendish post office, she could be the only person to see the rejection letters as they came in.

Her writing was becoming profitable, despite the rejections. Toward the end of 1899, she did a sort of personal inventory of what she considered her "assets." She saw her chief strong points as her writing ability and her steady conviction that eventually she *would* succeed. Besides her writing and her ambition, Maud also had quite a lot of money of her own for a twenty-five-year-old unmarried woman in 1899: three hundred dollars. Two-thirds of that came from her grandfather's will, but one hundred dollars was Maud's own savings, earned by writing.

Her very success was beginning to discourage her, however. When she wrote, instead of concentrating on the quality of her work, she found herself thinking about the money it would make. Sometimes she wrote "potboilers": melodramatic, unbelievable romances that were very popular and easy to sell among some publishers. Maud knew they were not great literature— but they *did* bring in money. Also, Maud knew that children's magazines liked stories with obvious morals, stories where bad children were punished and good children were rewarded. She had outgrown her fascination with the perfectly good child heroine Anzonetta Peters; she found real children, children who had fun and occasionally got into trouble, much more interesting. Those were the characters she wanted to write about, but couldn't, because no one would buy stories like that in 1899. Maud found the restrictions frustrating. She missed the days of writing simply because she loved to write, without a thought "of poking some dollars into my slim purse."

Also, back in Grandmother Macneill's strict household again, Maud had few people with whom to share her successes. Most of her old friends had moved away from Cavendish, or had married. Some had already died, which frightened her. Doctors in the late 1800s did not have the sophisticated medicines that we have today, so diseases like the flu often killed young, strong people—people like Herman Leard, who died suddenly in 1899. And in January of 1900, Maud received word that her father was dead. The news depressed her so deeply that she could not write for a long time. She had continued to exchange letters with her father, and he had been very proud of his daughter, the writer. There was no one else who appreciated her writing.

Maud had accomplished much, almost entirely on her own initiative. She had sent herself to college, if only for a year. She had established herself as a writer of popular and profitable stories and poems. But she was the only one of her kind in Cavendish, its sole authoress, and no one knew quite what to make of her. The neighbors viewed her work as an eccentric hobby for a young woman who, at twenty-five, was entering spinsterhood. Her grandmother, who disapproved of frivolity, made certain that her granddaughter kept her mind on important things like cooking and cleaning instead of celebrating her literary successes. If her published pieces brought her any sense of joy, there was no one she could share it with, no one who understood how important writing was to her, except of course her journal.

When a Canadian newspaper printed an article about Prince Edward Island poets, it listed Maud as "the foremost of the younger school of writers." She read it with mixed emotions. The honor was, she said, "the visible testimony of a place won for myself by hard toil." But she was alone with both the testimony and the toil.

Chapter

5

*I*n 1901 Maud heard from an old friend who knew that she was interested in writing. She'd recommended Maud for a job on the staff of a newspaper in Halifax, Nova Scotia: the *Daily Echo*. Maud was thrilled when she discovered that she'd gotten the job. "I'm a newspaperwoman!" she announced proudly.

That fall, Maud moved from her grandmother's house to a rented room in Halifax, and she began working for the *Daily Echo*. The position mainly involved proofreading. Maud would read the articles the men on the paper's staff had written, correcting mistakes in spelling, grammar, or style. By itself, that job would have been boring for a creative writer like Maud. But she soon found herself doing much more

In 1901 Maud set out for Halifax to be "a newspaper-woman."

besides proofreading. She called herself a "general handyman."

For instance, Maud began to write a column, "Around the Tea Table," which the *Echo* printed each Monday. It was full of light, innocent gossip and news—

"fun, fashions, fads, fancies," as Maud put it. Instead of using her own name when she wrote "Around the Tea Table," Maud used the pen name "Cynthia."

Maud also edited the society page in the *Echo*'s Saturday edition. The society page contained announcements of engagements, marriages, births, and visits of prominent people. Maud would clip information about these events from other local newspapers, then write them up for the *Echo*. When she first started this assignment, she tried to include funerals. And each week, the editor who checked her work "blue-penciled" the funerals: He crossed them out so they would not be printed. Maud was puzzled at first, then amused. "Evidently," she remarked, "funerals have no place in society." After that, she limited her society announcements to pleasant things. Even then, she sometimes had to be creative. If there were very few items for the society page, her editor simply ordered her to make some up!

Around Christmastime, the *Echo* sent reporters to the various local businesses that ran advertisements in the paper. The reporter would interview the owner or manager of the business and write up a brief review. Of course, the review was always favorable, because the *Echo* wanted to keep its advertisers. Maud was sent out on these assignments, which she disliked. One of the businesses she visited was a millinery—a hat shop—called Bon Marche. To Maud's surprise, soon after her review of the shop appeared in the paper, the milliner delivered a gift to her: a free hat!

Sometimes, in the *Daily Echo*'s hectic office, one page of an article, often the last page, would get lost. One

of Maud's many odd jobs was to rewrite endings for
these incomplete articles. It was one thing to complete
a news piece. In most newspaper stories, the final par-
agraphs are the least important; all the vital information is at the beginning. It was a challenge of a
different kind to make up an ending for a fictional
story. Yet Maud found herself doing that at the *Echo*,
too.

Many magazines and newspapers around the turn of
the century published serial stories. Each day, week,
or month, a new chapter would be added. The novels
of Charles Dickens, for example, were first published
as serial stories. Serials tended to be very long; the
more chapters the serial contained, the more the author
was paid.

The *Daily Echo* ran serial stories, too. Sometimes it
reprinted stories that had appeared in other publications. One of these was a British serial called *A Royal
Betrothal*. Quite a few episodes had already run when
the *Echo*'s editor discovered that the ending chapters
were missing. Knowing that Maud had written some
fiction, the editor gave her a new assignment: to create
an ending for *A Royal Betrothal*.

"My knowledge of royal love affairs is limited, and
I have not been accustomed to write with flippant levity
of kings and queens," Maud said of the assignment.
Also, Maud was used to writing short stories; serials
were more like novels, something Maud had not yet
attempted. Nevertheless, she dove into the new assignment with creative enthusiasm. Drawing on her experience with short stories, she deftly ended the long-
running serial.

Years later, Maud came across a copy of the entire story of *A Royal Betrothal*, complete with the original ending. It was, of course, very different from the one she'd written.

Maud did such good work with *A Royal Betrothal* that the next time her editor ran into trouble with a serial story, he gave her the assignment again. This time, he wanted to shorten a popular romance novel called *Under the Shadow* and use it as a serial. Several long, dull chapters had already run in the *Echo*. Maud was told to finish the serialization. She cut out all the descriptions and all the romantic parts, kept it short and interesting, and brought *Under the Shadow* to its conclusion.

Maud's work on *Under the Shadow* was reviewed in an unusual way. On her way to the office one day, soon after the final chapter had appeared, Maud happened to overhear a conversation between two women riding in a streetcar. One thing they talked about was the strange conclusion of *Under the Shadow*—how, after weeks of endlessly rambling episodes, it was suddenly and neatly wrapped up in eight chapters. As she listened, Maud could hardly keep from laughing out loud!

For all the work she did at the *Daily Echo*, Maud was paid five dollars a week. Even at that time that was a very low salary. To supplement her income, she taught part-time at a school in Halifax, helping Chinese immigrants learn English. Despite the low pay, Maud saw her newspaper job as at least a start, a stepping-stone into the world of professional journalism. Also, her position was something of an honor. She was the only woman on the *Echo*'s professional staff. Women generally worked for newspapers as secretaries or typists, not as editors or writers or even proofreaders. Few women in the early 1900s had the training or the ambition to enter the field of journalism. Besides, it was not considered "ladylike" to work for a newspaper, sharing an office with men and interviewing strangers.

Maud had not given up writing her own stories and poems, but she did discover that she had to change how and when she wrote. The day of a newspaperwoman was a long one. There simply was no time to write before or after work, so she tried writing during her breaks *at* work.

All her life, she had written under what she considered ideal conditions. She believed that she needed quiet and lots of uninterrupted time to do her best. When she began bringing her stories to her desk in the midst of the busy, bustling offices of the *Daily Echo*, she learned otherwise. If she had a few minutes between tasks, she was able to tune out all the activity around her and concentrate on her own project. And if she was interrupted—as she almost always was—she soon got used to picking up her writing again at any point, as if she'd never put it down. Even at home, she composed stories in her head while doing housework, then wrote them down when she had a chance.

But what she wrote during these snatched moments was further than ever from the "great literature" she dreamed of writing. Her days at the *Daily Echo* marked the height of Maud's sensational, romantic period. "I hate my 'pot-boiling' stuff," Maud lamented. She was sure that, given uninterrupted time and freedom, she could produce serious, high-quality literature.

Whatever Maud thought of her own writing, magazine editors—and, presumably, the magazines' readers—liked it. Gone were the days of struggling to sell a story. "Editors often *ask* me for stories now," Maud said proudly. As for those who had criticized her dream of becoming a writer, "the *dollars* have silenced them."

Much as she liked her job with the *Daily Echo*, Maud quit in June 1902. She could barely afford to live on her salary, while her grandmother was alone in the big old house in Cavendish. She decided that she was more needed there, and for the next nine years, she would not leave her grandmother's side.

Although Maud felt that it was her duty to stay with Grandmother Macneill, she did not necessarily enjoy it. Her grandmother had always been strict; in her old age, she was even more demanding and set in her ways. Maud was discouraged from inviting friends home, since they had to sit in the kitchen and be quiet, and the household was in bed by 9:00 P.M. After a year of living the independent life of a newspaperwoman, meeting new people and solving problems that even the men on the staff wouldn't touch, the transition was not an easy one. Also, she was approaching thirty, and she still wasn't married; it was unusual for a young woman to remain single for so long at that time, and her prospects of finding a husband and raising a family—things she wanted very much to do—dwindled each day she spent with her grandmother. After about only a year of living with Grandmother Macneill, Maud confided in her journal that she was afraid of becoming trapped in a suffocating way of life forever.

Maud's fame was growing, but she could only enjoy

that fame from afar. In 1908 she wrote a poem, called "Island Hymn," about Prince Edward Island. It was set to music by Lawrence Watson and adopted as a sort of unofficial anthem for the little province. The song was scheduled for its first performance at the opera house in Charlottetown in 1908. That evening, the composer and lyricist were called onstage for a bow. Maud wrote to a friend: "But only the composer could respond. The author couldn't go. She had to stay home and wish she could." Grandmother Macneill was not feeling up to the journey that evening. And Maud did not like to leave her elderly grandmother alone, especially if she was ill, so she chose to stay home.

More and more, Maud's social life was limited to letter writing. Luckily, the people she corresponded with were no ordinary, run-of-the-mill correspondents.

Chapter
6

One day Maud received a letter from Frank Monroe Beverley, a writer who lived in Virginia. He enjoyed Maud's stories and poems and wanted to correspond with her as a literary pen pal.

One of Frank Beverley's letters mentioned a woman from Philadelphia named Miriam Zieber, who had formed an informal writers' club. She believed that writers could learn about writing and improve their craft by corresponding with other writers. So she operated a sort of pen pal clearinghouse. She put aspiring young authors in touch with others who had similar interests, talents, and dreams. The correspondence between Frank Beverley and Maud never amounted to anything, but it put Maud in contact with Miriam Zieber, who was determined to match her with a compatible fellow writer.

The first pen pal Miss Zieber matched with Maud was Ephraim Weber, a thirty-one-year-old farmer who lived in Alberta, in western Canada. He was a member of a family of Mennonites, a very strict religious sect. The Webers were not well educated: They had never even heard of Shakespeare. Ephraim, however, loved literature and had dreams—what he called "the gleam"—of writing poetry. He'd already had a poem and an essay published when he began writing to Maud.

Mr. Weber was excited when he discovered that his pen pal was L. M. Montgomery. For quite a while, he had been reading the poetry and stories of L. M. Montgomery with great pleasure. Weber assumed that Montgomery was a man. He was disappointed when he learned that the "L. M." stood for "Lucy Maud," and that his new correspondent was a young woman. His first letter to Maud, dated March 12, 1902, was less than enthusiastic. But Maud did her best to prove to Mr. Weber that their correspondence *could* be worthwhile.

Maud had become quite successful at getting her poems and stories published. In 1902 alone, thirty of her pieces had been accepted. In 1904 she earned nearly six hundred dollars from her writing; in 1906, seven hundred dollars. At the time, this would have been an impressive salary for a man, while most women did not have any kind of paying job at all.

Maud knew the markets, too. Sometimes her work was still rejected by the first publication she sent it to, but instead of becoming discouraged, she simply sent the piece elsewhere until it was accepted. As a result, she was becoming familiar with many different magazines. She knew what all sorts of publications wanted and needed. When she wrote something, she generally had a good idea of which magazines would most likely be interested in it.

Maud was relatively young for a freelance writer. And she was teaching herself the complicated business of writing as she went along. Despite her disadvantages in the writing world, she was remarkably good at working with a wide variety of publishers.

In her letters, Maud explained all of this to Ephraim Weber. She critiqued his writing and recommended magazines that might consider it. She shared with him her experience as a budding author who was becoming successful.

As Ephraim Weber and Maud got to know each other better through their letters, they also began to reveal more personal information about themselves and their lives. Weber's letters were very intellectual and philosophical. Maud enjoyed a good intellectual challenge, and she liked to have someone to share ideas with. They would continue to write to each other for the next forty years.

After she was comfortably settled into her correspondence with Weber, Maud heard again from Miriam Zieber. Mrs. Zieber had another pen pal for Maud: George Boyd MacMillan, who lived in Alloa, a town in Scotland. For some mysterious reason, Maud was instructed not to tell Weber that she was also writing to MacMillan. She could, however, tell MacMillan about

Weber. Maud loved to write letters. Some of the letters she sent in her later years were forty pages long and had to be mailed in packages. So it was no great difficulty for her to write to both men.

Maud could rely on Ephraim Weber's letters to be intellectually stimulating. She could rely on George MacMillan's to be unpredictable and fun. Maud never knew what to expect when a package from MacMillan arrived in the mail.

Besides letters, MacMillan sent Maud little souvenirs of Scotland and of other places he traveled. Soon after they began writing to each other, Maud sent MacMillan a maple leaf—the symbol of Canada—and some rose leaves from her garden. In his answering letter, MacMillan sent Maud a sprig of heather, a plant symbolic of Scotland, and some other common Scottish flowers.

Maud enjoyed gardening. She grew flowers, not vegetables, and she especially loved the roses that flourished in her grandmother's yard. Flowers, Maud firmly believed, had souls. "I've known roses that I expect to meet in heaven," she said. From the earliest letters, Maud discovered that MacMillan shared her passion for growing flowers. Before long they were exchanging bulbs and plant cuttings in the mail.

When he learned of her love of the ocean, MacMillan sent Maud packages of seashells. And after a trip to Ireland, he mailed a rock chip from Blarney Castle, famous for its magical stone that, according to the legend, gave people "a way with words." After a few of these unusual packages had arrived, the customs officer on Prince Edward Island, who inspected incoming mail, drew Maud aside. What lunatic, he wanted to know, was sending her silly things like flowers and shells and pebbles!

Through George MacMillan, Maud was also able to keep up-to-date with books that were popular in England and the rest of Europe. And from Maud, MacMillan discovered new American and Canadian authors who were not yet popular overseas. MacMillan sent Maud two new, highly acclaimed British children's books: *The Secret Garden* by Frances Hodgson Burnett and Kenneth Grahame's *The Wind in the Willows*. In response, she told MacMillan about a young American author named Jack London and a rising Canadian poet, Robert Service. Both authors wrote about Yukon Canada and the gold rush in that cold northern territory, and Maud was partial to people who wrote about Canada.

Maud revealed much about herself and her interests in her letters to MacMillan. In one letter, she described herself. Maud Montgomery was five feet, five inches tall. Her hair had been golden blond when she was a child, but as she grew older, it darkened to a deep shade of brown. She usually wore it pinned up on top of her head: loose, it hung to below her knees. Like many members of the Montgomery family, Maud had unusual eyes: Her pupils sometimes grew so wide that her eyes appeared black instead of blue or gray. Maud felt that her hands were her best feature, for they were small and shapely. What she liked least about herself was her mouth. It was too small, she complained, and her teeth were not very healthy.

According to other people, Maud was lively, vivacious, and fun loving. This was indeed how she wanted people to see her: as outgoing and sociable and witty. When she was alone, however, she was often moody, and suffered from headaches and attacks of nerves. Sometimes she was unable to sleep for days at a time and paced her room night after night with insomnia. But few people knew about her problems. Even the friends who believed they were closest to Maud saw only what she wanted them to see. She was very good at covering up the dark side of her personality.

Maud enjoyed many hobbies besides gardening. One was photography. Cameras in the early 1900s were much more complicated than today's aim-and-shoot models. Taking a photograph involved carefully setting up a large, clumsy, rather heavy apparatus. Then the photographer had to prepare a set of glass plates with a chemical solution instead of simply loading a cartridge of film. Maud not only took her own photographs, she even furnished a little darkroom in her grandmother's house and developed her own pictures. Her favorite subjects were the places she loved best on Prince Edward Island.

Another of Maud's interests was astronomy. She owned a pair of binoculars and a chart of the constellations. On clear nights—which, on foggy Prince Edward Island, were rather uncommon—she observed the stars. In 1910 all eyes, binoculars, and telescopes were aimed at one object: Halley's comet. The comet is only visible to the naked eye for a few weeks every seventy-five years as it travels through the solar system, so Maud was eagerly awaiting a chance to see it. The sight disappointed her. "It was a sorry spectacle—little more than a dull white star," she said on May 23, 1910. A few years later, in 1918, she turned her binoculars toward another great astronomical sight: a nova, or exploding star. By that time Maud believed that there must be life on other planets. "It would be absurd to think God would waste so many good suns," she reasoned. She doubted, though, that human beings could learn *everything* about nature. "God," she said, "will always keep a few secrets to himself."

Since the sad episode of the kitten Pussywillow, Maud had owned a succession of cats, wherever she'd been living: Bobs and Topsy (who once followed her to church), Coco and Carissima, Max and Mephistopheles, Daffy and Firefly, Tom and Lady Katherine. In her old age, even Grandmother Macneill had overcome her aversion to cats as pets and actually enjoyed settling down with Maud's latest cat, Daffy, purring on her lap.

There were no stores near Grandmother Macneill's home. A shopping trip into the big city of Charlottetown was a rare event, something to be looked forward to and carefully planned, like a vacation. Because of this, Maud made much of what she needed herself. On Prince Edward Island in the early 1900s, homes were still lit by candlelight rather than by gas or electric lamps. Maud knew how to dip her own tallow candles, made from boiled animal fat. All summer, Maud and her grandmother enjoyed fresh fruit and vegetables from their garden and orchard, from Maud's uncle's farm nearby, and from the wild berry patches that covered the Island. When winter came, they enjoyed just as much what Maud had canned and preserved. Maud was also good at sewing both practical clothing and decorative embroidery; her patterns for handmade lace were well known in the Cavendish area and often won prizes at fairs.

Social life in Cavendish, and in most of Canada and the United States in the early 1900s, centered around the church. One evening a week there was a prayer meeting. "Prayer meeting is about the only amusement we have," Maud said as a teenager. Ten years later, that hadn't changed.

Maud was active in the Cavendish Presbyterian Church in other ways, too. Since she was a good cook, she participated in "pie socials." Girls baked their best pies and made them look attractive, then brought them to the church hall. Men at the social bid money for the pies, which were sold to the highest bidder. The person who bought the pie got to share it with the girl who had baked it. Maud also tended the flower arrangements that decorated the inside of the church; and, although she didn't like doing it, she still sometimes played the organ during services and directed the choir. Reluctantly, she also taught Sunday school classes.

Religion continued to fascinate her, just as it had when she'd wondered as a little girl where heaven was, or when she'd spent those fearful days waiting for the end of the world. But the Cavendish Presbyterian Church was very conservative, and it didn't give her answers to the kinds of religious questions she was asking. She especially wanted to know more about the afterlife, and began to investigate occult subjects like séances and reincarnation. She always insisted that she was skeptical of such things—that she didn't really believe in them, but was simply curious. Still, all through her life, in different ways, that curiosity about religion, the afterlife, and the occult would reappear.

These were just a few of the interests Maud wrote about to Ephraim Weber and George MacMillan in the many years of their correspondences. Both men were around Maud's age, and unmarried, when they began writing their letters. Intellectually, they were Maud's match—something she liked in her friends. The potential was there for a long-distance romance. But from the start, Maud made it clear that a romance was not what she was looking for. She wrote about emotional matters very freely, especially with MacMillan, and both men asked her for advice when they fell in love. But for the forty years she wrote to them, Maud never addressed them as anything but "*Mr.* Weber" and "*Mr.* MacMillan."

Despite a busy schedule of housework and community activities, letter writing and hobbies, Maud found—or made—time to write. One item that helped her when she was so busy was her writer's notebook. Whenever she had an idea she liked and wanted to remember so she could write about it later, she jotted it down in her notebook.

One of those random notes turned out to be far more important than Maud could have dreamed.

Chapter
7

*B*ack around 1895, Maud had scribbled an idea into her writer's notebook: "Elderly couple apply to orphan asylum for a boy. By mistake a girl is sent them."

Ten years later, Maud was looking for an idea for a serial story to sell to a Sunday school paper. She leafed through her notebook and found the note about the orphan and the elderly couple. It sounded like exactly what Maud needed for her story. Maud outlined a plot and gave the little orphan girl a name—Anne Shirley— and a personality—outspoken and imaginative. Maud even knew what her character looked like. She had seen a picture of a red-haired girl in a magazine. That, she decided, was Anne. Then Maud went to work on her story. She intended it to be only seven chapters long, just right for the Sunday school paper.

From the first, the orphan girl seemed to take on a life of her own. Anne's adventures and escapades quickly outgrew the limits of a seven-chapter short story. A character like Anne demanded more than just a few pages. She demanded a whole novel.

Maud had never written a novel. The idea of how much time and energy it would take to write one frightened her. But on a late spring evening, Maud sat down on the edge of her grandmother's kitchen table. She put her feet up on the sofa and propped a notebook

Maud began her most famous book, Anne of Green Gables, *in the kitchen of her grandmother's house.*

against her knees. The light of the setting sun coming through the west window fell onto the blank page before her. And Maud Montgomery started to write *Anne of Green Gables*.

Maud fell in love with Anne. She tried to make her "a real human girl," a child who could unrepentantly speak her mind, even if what she had to say shocked her elders. Maud put a lot of her childhood self into the character, and a lot of Cavendish and Prince Edward Island into the book's setting. She dedicated *Anne of Green Gables* to her parents. She knew how proud they would have been if they had lived to see their daughter's book.

All her life, Maud had been an astute observer of the people, places, and things around her. She incorporated many of her observations into *Anne*—but always with changes. Her characters seem very real, but they are based on combinations of people Maud knew, not just one person. People always wanted to know which person in Cavendish Mrs. Lynde, Matthew, or Marilla *really* was. Maud insisted that, with the one exception of Peg Bowen in the later novel *The Story Girl*, her characters came from her imagination, not real life.

The places in the book were also based on places Maud knew and loved on Prince Edward Island. The house she called Green Gables was very much like the home of her cousins, David and Margaret Macneill. Maud had sometimes visited the house as a little girl. In Maud's book, Cavendish was renamed Avonlea. The Lake of Shining Waters was a pond on Maud's uncle's property at Park Corner. The Haunted Wood was the place Maud and Well and Dave Nelson had told ghost stories about. Lover's Lane was a shady country road where Maud liked to walk when she needed time to think alone.

Things that had really happened found their way into the book, too: Mrs. Estey's liniment cake, the naming of plants and places and things. But Maud always made a few small changes. For instance, in *Anne of Green*

Many places around Cavendish found their way into Maud's books. One was a quiet country road that became Anne's Lover's Lane.

Gables, Anne longs for a dress with puffed sleeves, which her guardian, Marilla, will not let her have. As a child, Maud had wanted a hairstyle with bangs, which her grandmother wouldn't allow.

While she was working on *Anne*, Maud didn't tell anyone that she was writing a novel. She'd had lots of successfully published stories, but she still didn't have much confidence in her ability. She doubted that she'd be able to find a publisher who would be interested in her book. She had not changed much since her days of intercepting rejection letters in her grandparents' post office. She liked people to know about her successes, but she preferred to keep her failures secret.

Maud finished writing *Anne of Green Gables* in October 1905. Then she began typing it on her old, secondhand typewriter, which mangled capital letters and *w*'s. Finally, with hopes high, Maud sent her manuscript off to the first publisher. She'd chosen a new company because she had an idea that they would be more receptive to beginning novelists.

Anne returned, rejected.

Years of writing had made Maud used to rejection letters. She simply tried another publisher, this time an old, established one.

A second time *Anne* returned, rejected.

Four times Maud sent *Anne of Green Gables* to prospective publishers. Four times the manuscript was rejected. The first three publishers simply sent along a form letter, without any comments about what they thought of the book. But the fourth publisher included a personal letter. The letter said that *Anne of Green Gables* was good—but not good enough to publish.

That criticism discouraged Maud even more than a form-letter rejection. She packed her novel into a hatbox and stuffed it in a closet. She didn't throw it away. Maybe someday, she decided, she could edit it down to the short story it had been meant to be.

Anne sat in the hatbox in a closet for about a year. One day in 1906 Maud was housecleaning. When she reached the closet, she opened the hatbox and discovered her old novel. She reread it. It wasn't all that bad, she decided. Somewhere, there must be a publisher who would feel the same. Maud made a few revisions, and she invested in another typewriter—still secondhand, but at least it printed all the letters clearly. It also had a standard keyboard, something her old typewriter did not have. Typewriters were still fairly new inventions, and for several years different manufacturers used different arrangements of keyboards. So, while she was retyping her manuscript, she also had to learn how to type all over again.

Maud sent *Anne of Green Gables* to one more publisher: L. C. Page of Boston, Massachusetts. Two months later, on April 15, 1906, Maud received their response: They were interested in publishing her book!

Maud's fondest lifelong dream was about to come true. But in the midst of the excitement, she quickly discovered that being a published novelist and dealing with her publisher were going to be as difficult as writing—perhaps even more difficult.

The L. C. Page Company offered Maud a choice of how she would be paid for her book. The company could buy the manuscript outright for about five hundred dollars. Or Maud could receive a percentage of the price of every copy of the book sold—a royalty. Maud was not a businesswoman. And she doubted that *Anne of Green Gables* would be a best-selling, popular book. Nevertheless, she made a wise decision: She chose the royalties.

Some of the other decisions she made were not as shrewd. Maud never dealt with contracts when she sold stories or poems to magazines. A book, however, required a contract. She was anxious to get her novel published, and she worried that, if she disagreed too much with the terms of the contract, Page would decide not to accept *Anne* after all. So she signed a contract with some serious disadvantages in it for her.

Although Maud had been wise to choose a royalty agreement, the royalty rate she agreed to was low: 10 percent of the wholesale price of the book. The wholesale price is the amount the publisher charges, before the stores themselves mark the book up to make a profit. The wholesale price of *Anne of Green Gables* was ninety cents. With a 10 percent royalty, Maud would receive only nine cents from each book sold.

Maud also had to promise that she would write sequels to *Anne of Green Gables*, which would be published by Page. In addition, according to her contract, for the next five years Maud was obligated to write all her books for Page, all at the same low royalty. Even as she started writing the first sequel, Maud knew that she could not keep up her enthusiasm for Anne indefinitely. "I'm awfully afraid if the thing takes, they'll want me to write her through college," Maud predicted.

Then there was the matter of Maud's name. Maud wanted it to read "L. M. Montgomery." She had been using that name professionally, and she liked it. Her readers were familiar with it. L. C. Page, however, wanted to call its new author "Lucy Maud Montgomery." Maud had never liked her name "Lucy." She had never been called by it. She certainly did not want it to appear on the cover of her first book. Maud had settled for a low royalty. She had settled for many years of writing about the same character. But when it came to the question of her name, she would not back down. The author of *Anne of Green Gables* would officially be known as L. M. Montgomery.

Maud was thrilled when her copy of *Anne* arrived in the mail. "My book came to-day, 'spleet new' from the publishers," she crowed. She didn't particularly like the illustrations, which had delayed the publication date by several months. But to Maud, the book was like a newborn baby, and she couldn't help being excited.

Anne of Green Gables began to appear in bookstores in June 1908, selling for a retail price of $1.50 for a hardcover copy. The book was an immediate best-seller. By the end of the year, six editions—"I don't know the number of copies in an edition," Maud confessed—had been printed to keep up with the demand. When her first royalty check arrived in February 1909, it was for the monumental sum of $1,730.

Without a doubt, *Anne of Green Gables* was a sky-rocketing success, already destined to become a classic. But Maud was not altogether comfortable with her new fame and fortune. In a letter to Ephraim Weber, she proudly told him how much money she was making from her book, but asked him to keep it a secret.

Maud was proud of her first book's success—and a little surprised as well.

Suddenly, Maud was the celebrity of the little town of Cavendish. Magazines and newspapers in Canada, the United States, and England printed reviews of her book. Maud kept clippings of over sixty reviews, and almost every one said good things about *Anne*.

Maud was a little surprised at the response her book was getting. She had written *Anne of Green Gables* for children. She had expected its only readers to be teenage girls. Yet reviewers and readers were proving that *Anne* was popular among adults, too.

Maud was soon receiving fan mail from readers all around the world. She personally answered every letter she received—even when eighty-five letters from fans in Australia arrived on the same day. Some of the fan letters Maud received were not actually addressed to her. Instead, they were addressed to Anne, as if she were a real person, not a fictional character. One letter was sent to "Miss Anne Shirley, c/o Miss Marilla Cuthbert, Avonlea, PEI, Canada, Ontario." It arrived in Maud's mailbox, anyway. Another letter came for *Mr. L. M. Montgomery*. Its writer believed that Maud was his long-lost uncle, who'd had the same initials and had been an amateur author.

Every fan letter Maud received praised *Anne of Green Gables*. Children liked Anne because she seemed so realistic, with her overactive imagination that got her into trouble—and usually got her out of it, too. Many adults said they liked *Anne of Green Gables* because the book reminded them of their own childhood.

Maud was proudest of one very special letter. It was from a seventy-three-year-old author of books also enjoyed by both children and adults the world over: Mark Twain. In his letter to Maud, Mark Twain called Anne "the dearest, most lovable child in fiction since the immortal Alice" (meaning *Alice in Wonderland*). That was high praise from the man who had created characters like Tom Sawyer and Huckleberry Finn.

round the time that Maud was writing *Anne of Green Gables*, the Presbyterian church in Cavendish hired a new minister: Ewan Macdonald. He was originally from nearby Bellevue. His family, like Maud's, was of Scottish ancestry. He had black hair and dark eyes—and it soon became known that he was unmarried. Ewan was just a few years older than Maud. When he met her, he was immediately attracted to her.

At first, Maud was not very interested in Ewan Macdonald. He had a good education—far better than any of the young farmers of Cavendish—but whenever they talked Maud could see that he was not experienced in the kind of intellectual conversation she enjoyed. Still, she found herself liking him, since he was handsome,

In 1906 Maud became engaged to the Reverend Ewan Macdonald.

easy to talk to, and respected by his congregation— and he evidently liked her, since he spent so much time around the Cavendish post office! Maud was beginning to want the security and stability that marriage offered, and she dreamed of raising a family. She was no longer hoping or looking for love. She doubted that she would ever love anyone—including Ewan Macdonald—the way she had loved Herman Leard. Somewhat unromantically, Ewan Macdonald and Maud Montgomery began courting. In October of 1906, just as he was preparing to go to Scotland for a while to study, Ewan offered an engagement ring to Maud. She accepted his proposal.

Five years would pass before Maud and Ewan actually got married, however. Maud refused to leave her elderly grandmother, and Ewan was studying in Scotland. When he returned to the Island, his congregations were not near Cavendish. Then he accepted a church in Leaskdale, Ontario, a town on the mainland, not far from Toronto. Ewan and Maud saw little of each other during their long engagement.

Meanwhile, Maud was busy being a famous writer. She finished *Anne of Avonlea*, the first sequel to *Anne of Green Gables*, in 1908. She had started writing it almost as soon as her first book was accepted by the L. C. Page Company. Maud didn't think Anne was quite as interesting a character grown-up. The publication of Maud's second book wasn't as exciting for her as the first, either. It seemed more like an assignment from her publisher than a labor of love. Maud's readers, however, enjoyed the book. *Kilmeny of the Orchard*, based on one of Maud's serial stories, followed *Anne of Avonlea*. The L. C. Page Company, though, demanded more stories about Anne. Maud assured the publishers that she would write those stories—as soon as she'd finished another project.

In 1910 Maud was at work on a book called *The*

Story Girl. It was a collection of thirty-two stories told by a character named Sara Stanley. *The Story Girl* was Maud's personal favorite of all her books. In it, Maud was able to retell tales of old Prince Edward Island and all the romantic family histories she'd heard while she was growing up. She changed some names and invented a few situations to make the real stories more dramatic, but basically these were the ones she'd heard from Aunt Mary Lawson and other family members. A few years later, Maud wrote a sequel to *The Story Girl*. She called the second book of stories *The Golden Road*, and dedicated it to that wonderful storyteller in her life, Aunt Mary Lawson.

In the fall of 1910, Maud received an exciting invitation. The Page brothers, who owned the L. C. Page Publishing Company, wanted her to be their guest for a visit to Boston. Maud had never been to the United States, and she had never met George and Lewis Page, her publishers. That November she set out to spend two weeks in Boston, Massachusetts.

Maud's reactions were mixed. There was much to see in the big city of Boston. Maud enjoyed touring historical sites such as Lexington and Concord. And, though the tour was much too quick for her to see all she wanted to, she loved the Museum of Fine Arts.

Being a celebrity was fun for Maud, too. Nearly every evening there was one elaborate dinner or another for her to attend. Although she was a little uncomfortable around so many strangers, she had always enjoyed dressing up in pretty clothes and eating fine food. On her visit to Boston she was able to indulge in fancy dresses and excellent dinners to her heart's content. She even bought her first real evening dress for one of the dinners. But, in the midst of the big city and all the attention she was receiving, she was still the Maud Montgomery who appreciated the wonders of nature. As she was stepping out of a car for an evening of socializing, she happened to look up at the sky. The moon seemed to be passing behind a reddish shadow. In the middle of Boston, surrounded by women in stunning gowns and men in tuxedos, Maud stood watching a lunar eclipse.

Although Maud was impressed by some of what she saw in Boston, she considered Americans unnecessarily loud and boisterous. And she found that, now that she'd met them in person, she neither liked nor trusted the Page brothers, especially Lewis. Maud felt that she was not taken seriously or treated fairly by them, and she'd heard rumors that this was the way they treated women.

Maud had never considered herself a feminist. She had very traditional attitudes. She told an interviewer that a woman's place was in the home, and that her ideal was to be a wife and mother as well as a writer. But she did not like to see her rights ignored and violated just because of her sex. She wanted to receive the proper recognition for whatever she earned.

Women in Canada were demanding suffrage, the right to vote. Maud was independent, but she wasn't interested in politics, or in joining in the suffrage movement. Still, when Canadian women were finally able to vote in 1917, Maud was among them.

She believed that women should have rights and a voice in how they lived their lives. She didn't see women gaining that kind of power through politics, however. She believed that power, especially for women, came from a different source: education. In 1910 Maud found herself earning seven thousand dollars in royalties from her writing. This was at a time when a working woman in Canada brought home three hundred dollars a year, often less. She credited her success to hard work, perseverance—and a good education.

Those first years after *Anne of Green Gables* was published were stressful ones for Maud. The reaction of the little town of Cavendish to the new celebrity in its midst was not entirely positive. Some people were jealous of Maud's success. They belittled the amount of work she'd done and the disappointments she'd endured. Other people who had hardly spoken to Maud when she was Maud Montgomery, the post office keeper's granddaughter, were suddenly claiming that she was a close friend, now that she was a famous author. Maud did not like hypocrisy, and that sort of behavior bothered her.

Grandmother Macneill's health was also failing. Caring for the elderly woman and fulfilling her professional and social duties as a writer began to take their toll. Maud was often ill with migrainelike headaches. The young woman who had always loved good food now had no appetite. She suffered from insomnia and always felt tired. She knew she needed a vacation, but there was always her grandmother to think of.

Then, on March 10, 1911, after a bout of pneumonia, Grandmother Macneill died. Sometimes she may have seemed like an obstacle and a burden to Maud, but they'd lived together for a very long time, and Maud felt the loss keenly.

It was unheard of for an unmarried young woman to live alone; Maud's family would not allow her to remain in the big Macneill farmhouse so much as a week. Within days of the funeral, family members arrived to choose the things they wanted from Grandmother Macneill's belongings. Soon the house was empty and ready to be closed up. Maud went to live with her uncle John at Park Corner.

Four months later, on July 5, 1911, Maud married Ewan Macdonald. The ceremony took place right in Uncle John's Park Corner house. It was a small, quiet, practical ceremony. The recent death of Grandmother Macneill made a big celebration seem inappropriate. Besides, Maud was thirty-six. Ewan was forty, and a minister. People expected them to be somewhat sedate and dignified. Nevertheless, Maud, who loved pretty dresses, was not going to miss the opportunity to wear a beautiful wedding dress of ivory silk crepe and lace, with touches of chiffon and jewels. She carried a bouquet of white flowers—roses and lilies of the valley—and ferns. Around her neck she wore Ewan's wedding gift: a pearl and amethyst necklace.

The bride immediately liked the sound of her new name: Maud ("spelled *not* 'with an e' if you please") Macdonald.

An omen of bad luck troubled Maud that day. The wedding party found itself following a hearse mile after mile along Prince Edward Island's red roads. Maud would later realize that it was like a foreshadowing of problems to come.

Maud was married in her uncle's house at Park Corner.

The newlyweds were soon aboard a ship bound for Great Britain. Both Ewan and Maud were of Scottish ancestry, and they had decided to see their families' homeland on their honeymoon. Maud paid for the honeymoon trip out of her earnings from *Anne of Green Gables.* She also arranged for a very special tour guide: her Scottish pen pal, George MacMillan. Maud had never met the man who sent those odd parcels full of shells and stones and snips of plants, although she and MacMillan had been writing to each other faithfully for about ten years.

Maud loved the wild scenery of Scotland and the romantic old sites she, her husband, and MacMillan

Maud always loved pretty clothes. Her wedding and honeymoon provided a perfect opportunity for some new outfits!

visited. As a girl she had been fascinated by Sir Walter Scott's *Ivanhoe* and *The Lady of the Lake.* She had read about the places in those stories; now she was seeing them. Sometimes they met her expectations, but often she was disappointed; while the scenery was thrilling, Maud was always comparing it to Prince Edward Island. Next to the Island, she felt, Scotland and England were downright ordinary.

She enjoyed tramping around the many historic cas-
tles. But at one castle, it was not the history that moved
her, it was a little blue wildflower growing in the grass
around the castle walls. That same blue flower had
grown in the orchard outside Grandmother Macneill's
home. Maud had never seen a flower quite like it—
until now. Grandmother Macneill, who had been born
in England, must have brought the little plant with her
when she crossed the Atlantic, as a token of her former
home.

Maud introduced a Canadian custom to her Scottish
host during her visit. Any child who grew up on Prince
Edward Island knew that spruce trees oozed a sap that
could be chewed. When Maud found spruce trees in
Scotland, she shocked her friend MacMillan by popping
a wad of thick sap into her mouth. He had never tried
chewing spruce gum; he had never even heard of it.
And it was not a custom he intended to introduce to
the rest of Scotland. The gum, he complained, tasted
bitter.

After their travels around Scotland, Maud and Ewan
left George MacMillan and journeyed south, across the
border into England. Once again, Maud was thrilled
to see the places she'd read about and imagined for
so long: the Lake District where William Wordsworth
and Samuel Taylor Coleridge had written their poems,
the London of William Shakespeare and Charles
Dickens.

Maud also made a special trip to the little town of
Dunwich, in the county of Suffolk, England. That was
the village where Grandmother Macneill had been

born. Maud talked to a number of people, but no one seemed to remember her grandmother's family. Finally, Maud met a man who directed her to a small farmhouse: the house Grandmother Macneill had left so many years before to journey to Prince Edward Island.

Maud found a special souvenir in England, too. She still remembered the green-spotted china dogs on Grandfather Montgomery's mantelpiece—the ones that barked at midnight, according to her father. Maud wanted a pair of china dogs like her grandfather's to sit on the mantelpiece of her new home. She combed every antique store she saw in England, with no success. Finally, in a shop in the city of York, she found two matching china dogs. Their spots were gold, not green. And they were far too big to sit *on* the mantelpiece; they would have to sit on the hearth, one on either side of the fireplace. But they *were* spotted china dogs. Maud had never outgrown her habit of naming things; she called the dogs Gog and Magog.

After ten exciting weeks abroad, Maud and Ewan sailed back across the Atlantic to Canada. Ewan resumed his position as Presbyterian minister in the town of Leaskdale, Ontario, a rural community about fifty miles from Toronto, and in the neighboring parish of Zephyr. The church gave Ewan and his family a house in Leaskdale.

For the first time in her life, Maud had the responsibility of decorating her own home. It was a duty she thoroughly enjoyed. Before the honeymoon she had chosen colors and patterns of paint and wallpaper and

In York, England, Maud found the perfect china dogs for her parlor. She named them Gog and Magog.

carpets. She'd bought new furniture for all the rooms. When the Macdonalds finally settled into the Leaskdale Manse, everything was just as the new bride wanted it.

Whenever Maud had left her old home for any period of time, she'd suffered from homesickness for a while. Now she knew that she would not be going back to Prince Edward Island for a long time. And, with Grandmother Macneill gone, she had no home to go back to. Although Leaskdale was now Maud's home, she missed the Island. In the study where she would do

In Leaskdale, Ontario, Ewan and Maud lived in the manse, a home provided for them by Ewan's church.

her writing, she hung photographs of some of her favorite Island places, so that she would never be far from them in spirit.

One thing was still needed to make Maud's new home complete: a cat. When she got married, Maud had a cat named Daffy: a loud, independent creature. "Really, he's everything a cat should be, except that he hasn't one spark of affection in his soul," Maud said about her pet. Until the couple was settled in Leaskdale, relatives on Prince Edward Island had been taking care of Daffy. At last, Maud sent for him. He was packed into a pet carrier and placed on a train, unaccompanied. When Maud picked up the box at the train station, there were none of the expected yowls or meows. She was afraid to open the box, for she was sure that her noisy, active pet was dead. When Maud finally got up the courage to open the carrier, there was Daffy, very much alive, only a little shaken and frightened. He was soon investigating his new home, acting as if his dignity had been offended by the long, rough ride all alone. Daffy eventually forgave Maud and remained the manse cat for many years.

Those first years of her marriage were busy ones.

Maud owned a succession of cats, including Daffy.

"Yes, I understand the young lady is a writer," Ewan had said to his friends before the marriage. Now he was uncomfortable about the fact that his wife still wanted to publish her books under the name "L. M. Montgomery" rather than "Mrs. Ewan Macdonald." She had fought hard for the right to use that name, however, and she had no intention of giving it up. To Ewan's congregation, she would be "Mrs. Macdonald." To her readers, she remained "L. M. Montgomery."

The money Maud earned was welcome, so she could continue her writing, but Ewan expected her to be a housewife as well. She was also expected to fulfill all the duties of a minister's wife: attending the weddings and baptisms and funerals Ewan performed, hosting teas and church gatherings. With the money she made from her writing, Maud could afford to hire help with the cooking and housework, but she insisted that the servants eat their meals in the dining room, at the table with Maud and Ewan, and be treated like members of the family.

Despite all her new responsibilities, Maud continued to write. She rose early in the morning—six o'clock or earlier—and wrote by hand for a few hours. Typing was one of her afternoon tasks, and it took up much of her time. She considered hiring a typist, but only she could decipher the complicated maze of notes and arrows that made up her manuscripts. During the afternoons, Maud also set aside some time to take care of the business end of her work. Finally, she stayed awake far into the night to read. She reread the classic novels she'd enjoyed as a girl, but she kept up-to-date with the modern literature, too. And just for fun she

read a mystery novel or two. Still, there were gaps
between L. M. Montgomery novels after Maud got married. She did publish some books of short stories
around that time: *Chronicles of Avonlea* in 1912, *The
Golden Road* in 1913.

In 1912 a new role was added to Maud's duties as
writer, housewife, and minister's companion: the role
of mother. Maud's first son, Chester Cameron, was
born in July of that year.

Chapter 9

Maud had always wanted children. Her desire for a family was one of her main reasons for getting married. Now she had started a family with a baby boy. She wanted to name her first child Sidney Cavendish Macdonald, since her favorite name was Sidney, and she had sometimes used the pen name Cavendish, commemorating her hometown. Ewan, however, was not impressed by Maud's choice. So they compromised on the baby's name: Chester.

Maud intended to have a big family—at least six children. But she was nearly forty years old already, and she doubted that she would have as many children as she'd hoped. She was thrilled when she discovered that she was pregnant again in 1914. Meaning well,

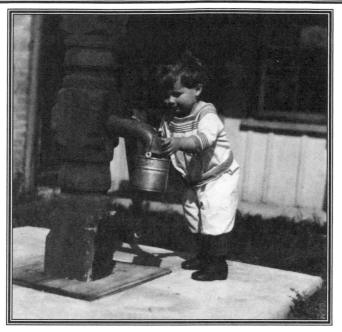

Maud's first child, born in 1912, was named Ches-
ter.

people had told her terrible things about pregnancy
and childbirth when she had been pregnant with Chester. But then, she had been healthy and comfortable,
and she had been able to ignore the terrible stories.
She expected the second pregnancy to be as easy. This
time, however, there were problems and complications.
Maud's second son, Hugh Alexander, was stillborn.

Maud was heartbroken at the loss of her baby. She
had talked about wanting a little girl instead of another
boy. Now she felt guilty.

Around the same time, a conflict that would escalate
into World War I was erupting in Europe. Canada
entered the war on the side of the Allies, along with

England and France. The principal opponent of the Allies was Germany. People in Canada acted to help their soldiers in Europe in any way they could. Maud got involved in Red Cross activities in Leaskdale, sewing, knitting, and preparing packages to send to the men overseas. Soon she was the president of the local Red Cross Society.

Many people were concerned about the war, but Maud took it personally. Every day, in her journal, she wrote about the war reports she had read in the newspaper. She agonized over the Allied defeats and rejoiced over their victories. The descriptions of the bloody battles haunted her. When Germany sank a passenger ship, the *Lusitania*, in the Atlantic Ocean in the spring of 1915, Maud cursed the German leader, Kaiser Wilhelm, in her journal: "May Wilhelm of Germany go down to the deepest hell haunted by the cries of the babes he has murdered and the women whose hearts he has broken!"

Most of the battles of World War I were fought with conventional guns, tanks, and grenades. Airplanes were used, but they were relatively new inventions. The atomic bomb was a weapon of the future, but chemical weapons almost as terrible were killing and maiming thousands of Allied soldiers. There was mustard gas, for instance—a chemical that burned the lungs and crippled as surely as a bullet or a bomb the young men it did not kill.

The more Maud heard about the war, the more she was obsessed with it, until she was even dreaming about it. One of her dreams came during a long and especially bloody campaign. The symbols in the dream seemed to say that the Allies would win. A few days later, the news arrived that the battle was over, and the Allies had been victorious. Maud, with her interest in the occult, began to believe that she could see into the future. She tried to interpret all her strange, obscure dreams and connect them to the progress of the war.

In 1915 what Maud needed, and needed badly, was a restful, relaxing vacation. She decided to go back to Prince Edward Island for a little while. It was the first time she had been home since her marriage seven years before.

Although Grandfather Montgomery was now gone, Maud's uncle and many of her cousins still lived at the old family home at Park Corner. These were the people she most wanted to see, and Park Corner was where she spent much of her time during the visit. But one moonlit night in June, Maud had an irresistible urge to walk down to the old Macneill house where she had grown up, and where her career as a writer had begun. Even in the darkness, Maud remembered the way.

The house had been closed up and abandoned for the seven years since Grandmother Macneill had died. It belonged to Maud's uncle now, but he had done nothing to take care of it, and it was in disrepair. The yard and the garden Maud had tended so lovingly were overgrown with weeds. Suddenly, the moonlight shone on the old, dilapidated house, and the years seemed to fall away. For a moment, Maud imagined that her grandparents were still alive, that she could walk in the door and up the stairs to her room, and she would be a child again. Then the dream faded with the moonlight, and she returned to her new family.

The vacation on Prince Edward Island did help Maud to cope with the problems in her life. She especially needed that restful time at her old home because she was pregnant again. After the death of her second baby, Maud had feared that she would not have another child. Still remembering her heartbreak over losing Hugh Alexander, she endured an anxious nine months. In October of 1915, Ewan Stuart was born—another healthy baby boy. The family called him Stuart.

Before long, however, the horrors of World War I returned to haunt Maud. Her half brother, Hugh Carlyle —Carl to his family—enlisted. He fought in the Battle

Stuart Macdonald was born in 1915.

of Vimy Ridge in 1917, where he was wounded and lay in the snow for eighteen hours before help arrived. As a result he lost a leg. Maud had never been close to her half brothers and sisters, but Carl, the youngest, was the most like his father, and Maud's favorite.

Maud's half brother Carl was injured in World War I. Here he is playing with Maud's younger son, Stuart.

In 1918 Maud took another vacation trip to Prince Edward Island. Chester and Stuart were now old enough to appreciate a visit to their mother's beloved home. They quickly became friends with their young cousins at Park Corner.

On this visit, Maud felt a compulsion to do something she had not been able to do three years earlier. She visited the old Macneill farmhouse again, and this time she went inside. The house was even more decayed than it had been the last time Maud had seen it, on that magical moonlit night when, for a moment, time had turned back. As she walked through the empty, dusty rooms on creaking floors, Maud had a strange sensation that the house was haunted. She knew that she should leave and never return. And this *would* be her last visit. In 1920 the old Macneill home was torn down.

Maud was busy with all the duties of a minister's wife, she had two young children to care for, and she was doing her part in the war effort. But her many activities did not prevent her from writing. In 1915 she published *Anne of the Island,* the second successor to *Anne of Green Gables.* This latest book was about Anne in college.

Maud's contract with the L. C. Page Company ran out with the publication of *Anne of the Island.* The war had made Maud more conscious than ever of being a Canadian. She wanted to be represented by a Canadian publisher now, at least for the editions of her books that were printed and sold in Canada. She chose the publishing company of McClelland, Goodchild and Stewart. Meanwhile, she continued to look for an American publisher other than L. C. Page.

Her first project with McClelland, Goodchild and Stewart was very Canadian. It was also something that the L. C. Page Company had refused to accept. Maud had been writing quite a lot of poetry, especially since Canada had entered the war. She put together a volume of her poetry, which she called *The Watchman*, and dedicated it to the Canadian soldiers.

Maud's books about Anne had made her famous worldwide, but her many fans knew little about the books' author. So in 1917 *Everywoman's World*, a popular Canadian magazine for women, contacted Maud. The editors wanted her to write a piece about her life and her career. The magazine would print the autobiography as a serial in six sections.

Maud's response was an essay she called "The Alpine Path." That title was from "The Fringed Gentian," a poem about a mountain wildflower. Maud could no longer remember its author, but she had loved it as a girl and had kept a copy of it on the inside cover of her school notebook as an inspiration.

"The Alpine Path" article began with Maud's recollections of her childhood. She described all the events in her life that had influenced her becoming a writer, including the *Marco Polo* essay, the poem about Cape LeForce, Dalhousie College, the year with the *Halifax Daily Echo*. Maud concluded the piece with the publication of *Anne of Green Gables* and her marriage.

She was surprised to hear from the magazine soon after she turned in the article. The editors liked the piece. But they wondered if Maud might expand it a little. What they wanted, specifically, were an extra thousand words on Maud's romantic relationships.

Like so many popular magazines today, *Everywoman's World* knew that its readers wanted to find out something personal about the people they read about in its pages. Maud, however, chose to keep the private aspect of her life private.

There was much about Maud's life that no one knew. She was miles away from the people she had grown up with and she could not have confidantes among the people in her husband's congregation. She wrote letters constantly, and often friends and family visited for short periods, but she had no close friend she could talk to about her problems and worries.

And Maud did have problems and worries. To begin with, she had mixed feelings about being the wife of a minister. She had always been high spirited and fun loving, enjoying music and parties with dancing. Ewan's congregation, however, would not consider it appropriate for the minister's wife to indulge in worldly, frivolous things like popular music and dancing. Maud had been thrilled when the Macdonald family acquired a Victrola, an early kind of record player. But she was careful to play her records—except the classical ones—very quietly, so the neighbors wouldn't hear and disapprove. She enjoyed good conversation, and even a bit of gossip, but she noticed that people watched what they said when she walked into the room—again, because she was the wife of the minister. Ewan, busy with his work and convinced that children were a mother's responsibility, left the task of raising Chester and Stuart almost entirely up to Maud. The two boys even learned about God and religion, not from their father the minister, but from their mother. Maud

Maud tried to portray the image of a good minister's wife—but inwardly rebelled.

was so frustrated, she once wrote to George MacMillan: "Those whom the gods wish to destroy they make ministers' wives."

Maud did have one special confidante: her cousin, Frederica Campbell. Frederica, or Frede, as she was called, was several years younger than Maud. She was one of the Park Corner cousins and had usually been there when Maud visited. As children, the two girls had little to do with each other, but as Frede grew up, Maud began to see that she and her younger cousin were very similar, and they became good friends. When Maud heard that Frede wanted to go to college, she paid her cousin's tuition from her earnings. Frede studied home economics, then taught at a women's college. The two women exchanged letters often. Whenever she had the opportunity to visit, Frede was a welcome guest in the Macdonald household.

One of the interests Maud and Frede shared was a fascination with the occult. The cousins sometimes asked questions of a Ouija board, whose mystical pointer was supposed to move by supernatural power to spell out answers. Maud was skeptical of the Ouija board. She said that the only power moving the pointer was the person sitting at the board. Nevertheless, whenever Maud used the board, answers would be misspelled in ways that had special meanings for her. And the answers sometimes revealed things about her marriage that Maud had never told anyone. At other times, Maud and Frede tried to make tables knock and move around the room by themselves. Since Maud was the minister's wife, however, they decided to stop dabbling so visibly with the occult, especially when rumors began to spread around town about prominent women trying to contact the devil.

Maud and Frede also talked about ghosts and spiritualists, or mediums—people who claim to be able to contact the dead. Maud found the idea hard to believe, especially when she noticed that the mediums always seemed to contact kings or queens or famous writers, never ordinary housewives or laborers.

While Maud was skeptical about many aspects of the occult, she and Frede _wanted_ to believe that some of the exciting ideas about ghosts, a sixth sense, reincarnation, and premonitions might be true. Maud was too analytical and too critical to accept these phenomena without proof, so she and Frede agreed to conduct an experiment. If Maud died first, she promised to contact Frede from the afterlife. If Frede died first, she would somehow contact Maud.

In 1919 Maud received an urgent message to come to Frede's college. An epidemic of influenza called Spanish flu had struck North America, and thousands of people were ill. Maud had recently had the Spanish flu herself and had recovered. Frede had also contracted the flu, but instead of getting better, she developed pneumonia. There was no effective way for doctors to treat pneumonia; since antibiotics had not yet been invented, it was usually fatal. When Maud reached the college, Frede was dying, and at dawn one cold January morning, she died with Maud by her side.

For weeks Maud waited for some sign from Frede that there _was_ an afterlife and that the spirits could communicate with the living. But no sign came. After that sad, failed experiment, Maud began to turn her trust to rational science.

There was another reason Maud wanted to avoid thinking too much about the afterlife. Ewan was becoming more and more obsessed with the subjects of death and hell. After they were married, Maud had discovered that Ewan suffered periodically from severe depression, and when he was depressed he talked about hell. That year, 1919, was especially bad for him.

Depression was not understood or accepted in 1919. Maud wanted to do all she could to help her husband, but she also knew that she had to hide Ewan's condition from his congregation. So Ewan quietly went on a vacation to Massachusetts to visit with his sister and to rest and relax. While there, however, his condition worsened. Maud left Chester and Stuart with her trusted housekeeper and rushed to be with her husband. She found him in the depths of a dark depression, sometimes sitting in gloomy silence, sometimes ranting that he regretted ever having a family, that a terrible hell awaited all of them. After many desperate weeks, Ewan was finally well enough to return to his home and his work.

Somehow, despite all the unhappiness around her, Maud was still writing about her cheerful heroine, Anne. In 1917 she had written *Anne's House of Dreams*, in which Anne and Gilbert Blythe are newlyweds. The year that Frede died and Ewan was so severely depressed, 1919, saw the publication of *Rainbow Valley*, about Anne and Gilbert's children.

That year Maud also went to the theater to see a movie version of *Anne of Green Gables*, produced by Realart Pictures. In 1919 filmmakers were working on a way to include sounds and voices on the film, but the process was not yet perfect, so this first film version of *Anne of Green Gables* was a silent movie. Important dialogue appeared printed on the screen.

The movie disappointed Maud for several reasons.

One reason was financial. In 1919 Maud was involved in a lawsuit with the L. C. Page Company. To settle with them, she sold them the dramatic rights to her work, as covered in her contract. These included the rights to adapt her novels as plays or films. The L. C. Page Company received forty thousand dollars for the film rights to *Anne of Green Gables* when it was made into a movie. Half of that money would have been Maud's if she had not chosen to turn over the dramatic rights.

Besides that, the filmmaker had taken many liberties with Maud's story. Maud's book is full of images of Prince Edward Island. It has a distinctly Canadian flavor. But the film seemed to be set in New England, in the United States. An American flag could be seen flying over the schoolhouse in one scene. "Crass, blatant Yankeeism!" cried Maud. The filmmaker also made up adventures for Anne that Maud had not written. One adventure involved a skunk—and there are no skunks on Prince Edward Island.

Finally, Maud was disappointed with the young actress cast as Anne: Mary Miles Minter. Mary Miles Minter was a popular child star of the time, and a competent actress, but too ladylike and delicate to portray feisty Anne.

Meanwhile, Maud was at work on a book called *Rilla of Ingleside*. Rilla is Anne and Gilbert's daughter. With *Rilla of Ingleside*, Maud was certain that she had no more to say about Anne. "I am done with *Anne* forever," wrote Maud. "I swear it as a dark and deadly vow. I want to create a new heroine now."

Writers often get tired of even their favorite characters. Sir Arthur Conan Doyle, who created Sherlock Holmes and his mysteries, tried after many stories to kill Holmes so that he would no longer have to write about him. But the public demanded more Holmes, and Doyle had to continue to write his stories. Eventually, reluctantly, Maud would also have to return to Anne.

But for the time being, Maud was infatuated with her "new heroine," Emily Starr. *Emily of New Moon* was published in 1921. Like Anne Shirley, Emily is remarkably similar to Maud in many ways. For instance, she dreams of becoming a writer and uses letter-bills— the colored scrap paper from the post office—to write long letters to her father, who is dead. Maud had sometimes written letters like these to her dead mother. *Emily of New Moon* was immediately praised as Maud's best book since *Anne of Green Gables*.

Before long Maud was not just a popular author, she was also an honored and distinguished author. In 1923 the Royal Society of Arts of England invited her to become a member of that prestigious literary society. She was the first Canadian woman to receive and accept such a commendation.

This celebrity gave Maud opportunities to do some traveling. Various organizations around Canada and the United States invited her to come and lecture, or to read aloud from her books. When these trips didn't take her too far away from her family for too long, she accepted the invitations.

The Macdonalds sometimes vacationed as a family, too. During the summer of 1924 they took a trip to the United States. One of their stops was at Mammoth Cave

in Kentucky. Maud and Ewan, Chester and Stuart went
far underground to the caverns' wonderful, beautiful
chambers. Maud expected the caverns to be cold. Instead, they were relatively warm (fifty-four degrees
Fahrenheit), and breezy as well. The place kindled her
imagination, making her think of the "old gods of the
underworld."

On the trip back to Leaskdale, the family stopped
at Niagara and Horseshoe falls, on the border between
Canada and the United States. Artificial floodlights il-
luminated the American side of the Falls. That evening
there was a tremendous thunderstorm, and the light-
ning set the Canadian side of the falls ablaze with nat-
ural floodlights. This impressed Maud far more than
the gaudy, electric American version.

One persistent problem haunted her, however, even
when her professional and personal lives seemed to be
going well. For a long time, despite the fact that she
had a new publisher, Maud had been fighting with the
L. C. Page Company. Breaking away from them com-
pletely was not going to be easy. In fact, it had led
Maud to court.

rom the beginning, Maud had never felt comfortable with the Pages. Almost as soon as *Anne of Green Gables* was accepted, Maud had suspicions and questions about them and their company.

The years had taught her the answer to her questions. Beginning writers may receive a relatively small royalty, or percentage of the price of each book sold. As they become established and write a number of popular, best-selling books, they receive a higher royalty. Maud had written many successful books: the *Anne* series, *The Story Girl*, *Emily of New Moon*. Yet she was still being paid the same low royalties that she had been offered for *Anne of Green Gables*, her first novel. When the Pages had entertained Maud in Boston, she had tried to bring up the subject of higher royalties. But they were firm in their offer. Maud had not yet been confident enough to argue.

There were other problems besides the disagreement over money. Maud had felt stifled by the publisher's demands for one Anne book after another. And there were personal stories about Lewis Page himself that had made Maud uncomfortable. Other authors who had worked with him told Maud confidentially that they suspected Page gambled away quite a bit of the money he made from his writers, and that he had an eye for attractive women.

Maud the new author had been thrilled to get *any* reputable publisher interested in her work. Maud the established author, who understood more about the business of writing, knew that she had not been treated properly after over ten years of success.

Maud's break with the L. C. Page Company had begun in 1916, when Maud decided to publish *The Watchman*, her volume of poetry, with a different company. Then, in 1917, the Frederick Stokes Company had expressed an interest in *Anne's House of Dreams*. Stokes offered Maud an advance of twenty-five hundred dollars. An advance is money given to an author before a book is published—often before the book is even finished. It represents part of the book's royalties. More than that, it is a sign of the publisher's faith that the book will be successful. Even today, a twenty-five-hundred-dollar advance for a children's book is hardly shabby. By the standards of 1917, it was a handsome sum.

Maud signed a contract with Stokes. One of the terms

of the contract was that Maud could not publish anything new about Anne with any other company. Since Maud was getting tired of the character—and of Page—she agreed.

When the L. C. Page Company became aware that Maud had defected to another publisher, its first reaction was to threaten a lawsuit against her. Page claimed that a mistake had been made on the royalties of one printing of *Anne of Green Gables*, and that as a result, Maud had been overpaid one thousand dollars. Now, said the publisher, she would have to give the money back.

Maud had recently joined an organization for writers called the Authors League of America. One service the league provided to its members was legal counsel. Determined to fight Page, she quickly contacted the league for an attorney. "*They* have discovered *me* to be a woman whom they cannot bluff, bully, or cajole," Maud said firmly.

It would not be the first time Maud had been involved in a lawsuit. Once, while reading a magazine, she had noticed a poem that sounded very familiar. The poem was hers—but, according to the name printed in the magazine, the poet was someone else. Maud was flattered that someone had found one of her poems good enough to plagiarize, but she was not about to let the plagiarism go unnoticed or unpunished. She sued and won. Maud had also brought an earlier lawsuit against Page. In the first edition of one of her books, *Kilmeny of the Orchard*, a whole chapter was missing. All the later printings were corrected and the person responsible for the mistake was fired, but Maud also sued for damages. Maud had made herself very familiar with the law as it applied to authors.

She was determined to win her latest lawsuit, but she had to do it quietly. A minister's wife who was not supposed to dance or play popular music or enjoy parties or gossip was certainly not supposed to go to court. Both Maud and the L. C. Page Company expected a speedy trial. But both sides underestimated the other's stubbornness.

At first the only issues were the thousand-dollar mistake and a question about rights to reprint the existing Anne books. Maud held her ground. She thought everything was settled when Page bought the rights to the books she'd published with them, paying her eighteen thousand dollars. At that time they also acquired the dramatic rights to her work. Finally, Page wanted to publish one last book by Maud: a collection of some of her old short stories. It sounded innocent enough. Maud agreed.

But, as things turned out, the case was far more complicated. Over the years, Maud had submitted a number of short stories to Page. Many of the stories, although not all, were about Anne or other characters who lived in Avonlea. Some of the stories were finished; others were mere sketches or ideas. Back in 1912 the L. C. Page Company had asked Maud to polish some of those short stories for publication in the book *Chronicles of Avonlea*. The stories not used in that book were sent back to Maud—or so she believed. She didn't know that her unscrupulous publisher had kept copies of them. Just as she was preparing to send the Pages some of her old stories for the final book, according to the terms of the agreement, they informed her that they had found copies of her work in their vaults. *Those* were the stories they wanted to publish. In 1920, L. C. Page announced that it was releasing a new L. M. Montgomery book: *Further Chronicles of Avonlea.*

Maud was furious. First, the stories were just drafts, needing extensive editing and revision. Second, like any writer, Maud sometimes tried using an idea for a story in many different ways before she settled on the best version. Some of the stories in *Further Chronicles* were drafts that she had discarded so she could use their main ideas elsewhere. Because of this, many of the stories in *Further Chronicles* seemed to repeat episodes in her other books. This could be confusing and annoying for Maud's readers. Finally—and worst— some of the stories mentioned Anne. The L. C. Page Company was even implying that *Further Chronicles* was another Anne book. The illustration the publisher wanted on the cover of the book showed a red-haired girl who looked like Anne. This violated Maud's new contract with Stokes.

So Maud found herself back in court.

The trial was an enlightening experience for Maud. She again found that the L. C. Page Company expected to take advantage of her because she was a woman. She began to hear from Page's former clients. They told Maud that the Pages often tried to intimidate their women writers into accepting inferior terms. The truth also came out about how *Anne of Green Gables* had *really* been accepted for publication. When the manuscript first arrived at the publisher's offices, the Page brothers intended to reject it. But one girl on the staff was originally from Prince Edward Island, and she liked the story. Another person on the staff also thought that it was good. These two people were the reason *Anne of Green Gables* was published by the L. C. Page Company. George and Lewis Page had very little to do with it.

All through the summer of 1920 the trial dragged on. Maud spent that time either in Boston or on a train traveling between Boston and Canada. She was told that she made an excellent witness, because she remained calm while she was being questioned. Even some experienced businessmen had broken down on the witness stand. Little did Maud's attorney know that, after a day in court, she went up to her hotel room and cried.

Nine years would pass before the case was entirely settled. The final decision was in Maud's favor.

After the trial, when the expenses on both sides were tallied, Maud found that she had won a total of three thousand dollars. But more important was the satisfaction she had gotten by proving that a woman could take on the L. C. Page Company and win. She still could not think of herself as a feminist, but she did not like to see powerful businessmen take advantage of women, either.

The lawsuit also made Maud aware of how far she had come, financially, as a professional writer. Little had she known, back in 1896, when she'd been excited about her first three-dollar payment that her career to date would have earned her close to seventy-five thousand dollars.

The Macdonald family—Maud (with child), Stuart, Ewan, and Chester—looked close and content, but their private life was far from perfect.

Chapter

11

By 1926 Ewan had been Leaskdale's Presbyterian minister for fifteen years. That year, however, there were changes afoot in the small community that would affect Ewan and Maud.

Throughout Canada, Presbyterian congregations were joining with Methodists and Congregationalists to form a new church, which called itself the United Church of Canada. Ewan's churches in Leaskdale and Zephyr were very unsettled by the new movement. The dissent in the community made life difficult for the Macdonalds. When additional problems arose, Ewan began to think about moving to a less demanding parish.

It did not take him long to find a new congregation

in Norval, Ontario, a small farming community not far
from Leaskdale.

The Macdonalds moved into the big, comfortable
Norval manse and life continued very much as it had
in Leaskdale. Maud found herself involved in many of
the same kinds of activities. There were the usual
church-related women's groups and meetings Maud was
expected to host. Of course, Maud was a regular member of any local literary society. And she continued to
enjoy music and theater, in ways that were acceptable
for the wife of the minister.

Maud liked working with young people, even though
she often complained that modern young people just

*Ewan's second congregation was in Norval, Ontario. Once
again, the Macdonalds lived in the manse.*

weren't as intelligent and interested in participating and learning as they had been when *she* was a girl. One of the jobs she took on when she arrived in Norval was the direction of a youth theater. In this venture, sometimes the independent-thinking, outspoken Maud was put in the difficult position of dealing with censorship. No matter what her own feelings were, she was expected to "clean up" anything in a performance that the community might find offensive. In one play that Maud's group performed, there was an important scene in which a female character had to climb in a window. There was no way a woman in a skirt could climb in a window without revealing a bare leg. For a young lady to show her bare leg was considered immodest, even immoral, in rural Canada in the 1920s. Maud knew that the Norval audience would disapprove of the scene. So she assigned the female role, not to a girl, but to a young man. His bare legs also showed as he climbed in the window—but a man's legs were more acceptable.

During her years at Norval, Maud's worldwide fame and recognition grew. In 1927 the prime minister of Great Britain, Stanley Baldwin, was traveling through Canada. Prince Edward Island was one of the places he visited on his tour. He had a special fondness for the little province, he said, because of one of his favorite books: *Anne of Green Gables*. Now that he was on the Island, he hoped to meet the book's author. In fact, Maud *had* just been visiting the Island, but had already returned to her home in Norval. She would, however, get another opportunity to meet her important fan.

Prime Minister Baldwin was in Canada to celebrate the fiftieth anniversary of Canada's Confederation, when it became a united country. Edward, the prince of Wales—the son of the king of England and the first in line to inherit the throne—was also on hand for the festivities. Because she was such an important figure in Canadian literature, Maud was invited to a party in Ottawa, Canada's capital, to meet the prince. Of course, she accepted the honor. Once, as a struggling young writer trying to complete someone else's story, Maud had complained that she knew nothing about British royalty. Now she was meeting a member of the royal family! She was excited about being introduced to the prince of Wales, but he didn't seem especially enthusiastic about her work. Fortunately, Prime Minister Baldwin was at the same party. He and Maud finally met, and they spent an enjoyable evening discussing their favorite books.

There were awards in store for Maud, too. The Literary and Artistic Institute of France presented Maud's books with the Silver Medal of Literary Style. And in 1935 King George V of England made Maud an officer of the Order of the British Empire—a high honor, especially for a woman and an author for young people.

Meeting her famous fans was exciting. But in 1928 she had the opportunity to meet someone even more special. He was not famous or world-renowned, but he was someone whose life and work Maud had known and enjoyed for a long, long time—twenty-six years. She finally met her original literary pen pal, Ephraim Weber.

The first meeting was a brief one. Weber and his wife

were driving through the eastern part of Canada and visited the Norval manse. Then, in 1930, Maud traveled to western Canada. She returned to Prince Albert and to the places in Saskatchewan she had known as a teenager. During that trip, Maud saw her father's grave for the first time. That was a sad and emotional experience for her. She still missed her father and the pride he took in her writing.

While she was in the western provinces, Maud also dropped in on Ephraim Weber, who was teaching at a school in Saskatchewan. During her visit, Weber invited Maud to read aloud to his students and autograph copies of her books. This delighted the girls, who loved *Anne of Green Gables* and *Emily of New Moon*. The last meeting between Weber and Maud was in Toronto, where the Macdonalds were living in 1935.

Maud continued to share good news with her other pen pal, George MacMillan, too. She had been disappointed by the 1919 film of *Anne of Green Gables*, but in 1934 a new movie based on the book was released by RKO, one that she liked much better. In fact, Maud saw the film four times. And of course she wrote about it in a letter to MacMillan. When the movie was screened in Scotland, MacMillan wrote back to Maud that he had also seen it—seven times!

A young actress named Dawn Paris played the role of Anne. Dawn Paris also used the professional name Dawn O'Day. Dawn was so impressed by the character she played in *Anne of Green Gables*, she changed her name again. This time she began calling herself Anne Shirley, after her favorite role. She kept that name throughout her future acting career, which included a second appearance as Anne in the 1940 film *Anne of Windy Poplars.*

Maud had vowed never to write another word about Anne, and although she'd liked Emily when she had written about her in *Emily of New Moon,* she again seemed to lose interest when faced with writing sequels. She felt it was time to invent some new characters.

One of them was a precocious little girl named Marigold. *Magic for Marigold* was based on a serial story Maud had written for a magazine. She also created a new adolescent heroine, Pat Gardiner, who was featured in two books, *Pat of Silver Bush* and *Mistress Pat.* Then, in the mid-1930s, Maud started working on *Jane of Lantern Hill.* Jane Stuart is a girl determined to reunite her estranged parents. Maud had a sequel in mind for *Jane of Lantern Hill,* but never finished it.

Maud was at her best when she was writing for children, and about children—about the funny but realistic escapades they got themselves into and out of. She recognized that her skill was a special talent, a gift. She also knew that her unique talent was needed, because there simply was not a lot of quality literature for young people. So she continued to work for this audience.

Still, Maud felt that the only way to be remembered as a great writer was to publish a serious piece of literature for adults. She wrote two novels for an adult audience around this time. *The Blue Castle* is a romance about an unattractive woman who traps a husband by convincing him that she has only a year to live. Though most of Maud's earlier stories had taken place on Prince Edward Island, *The Blue Castle* is set in Ontario. Maud's other adult novel, *A Tangled Web*, is a sort of mystery involving the inheritance of a vase.

Despite the new books and new characters, Maud's readers still loved Anne the best. Finally, she gave in to public demand and produced two more books about her. *Anne of Windy Poplars*, which consists of love letters between Anne and Gilbert, was published in 1936. When an edition of the book appeared in England, it was quickly named "the romantic book of the month" by the British newspaper the *Daily Mirror*. Two years later, *Anne of Ingleside*, about Anne and her babies, was published. *Now*, Maud hoped, she was truly free of Anne Shirley Blythe, and she could move on to other things.

What Maud could not break free from were the painful difficulties in her own life. Ewan's bouts of depression continued to come and go, though again his condition was kept as secret as possible from his new congregation and the community. He also suffered from a variety of physical ailments. Sometimes the stress was too much for Maud. Physically and emotionally exhausted, she was also prone to illness and relied on tranquilizers to help her relax. She continued to keep hidden her frustrations at the restrictions placed on a minister's wife.

Nevertheless, Maud found enough in her life to enjoy. The Macdonald family was quick to acquire the latest inventions, from the Victrola to the automobile, for Maud appreciated modern conveniences. For years, too, she had been a popular lecturer. So, when an opportunity arose for Maud to combine her experience as a public speaker with her curiosity about new technology, she eagerly accepted the challenge. In 1931 Maud was invited to participate in a live radio broadcast. She chose to read some of her poems on the air, reaching many more people than she would have in person, even in the largest lecture hall.

As a young woman on Prince Edward Island, Maud had become interested in photography and darkroom developing, and she never lost her fascination with the camera. She was not a professional, but her work was considered very good for an amateur. So when Kodak, the film and camera company, sponsored a photography contest, Maud was asked to be a judge. In appreciation for her services, she was given another exciting gadget from the world of modern technology: a movie camera. She had already snapped hundreds of still pictures of her family and the Canadian countryside. With her new toy she began to shoot reel after reel of scenes of Norval and Prince Edward Island.

Meanwhile, Chester and Stuart were growing quickly into active, bright young men. The Macdonalds tended to worry more about Chester than about Stuart. Chester was intelligent—but always a problem. First there was some concern that he was developing symptoms of tuberculosis, the disease that had killed Maud's mother. It was a false alarm, fortunately. Then he nearly lost an eye in an accident. Stuart, meanwhile, was making a name for himself in athletics. He was a skilled competitive gymnast; for two years he was the junior gymnastics champion of the province of Ontario. In 1933 he carried off a national title as well.

Unfortunately, around the same time, Ewan's condition again took a turn for the worse. Now, besides being depressed, he seemed to be losing his memory. It became impossible for him to continue in his position as minister. After nine years at Norval, Ewan resigned in 1935 and retired.

Once again, the Macdonald family was moving, this time to a house set on a hillside in the city of Toronto. Maud never tired of giving things names, and her new home was no exception. It was called Journey's End.

Chapter 12

Not long after the Macdonalds moved to Toronto, Maud heard news from Prince Edward Island. The government was buying the farmhouse that belonged to David and Margaret Macneill, Maud's cousins, the house that had been the model for Green Gables. It was within the borders of the newly created Prince Edward Island National Park. Rather than demolish it, the government had decided to make it a park attraction. Many tourists had already traveled to the Cavendish area, hoping to see the places they'd read about in *Anne of Green Gables*. Now there would be a place they could walk into and enjoy.

The old farmhouse would be furnished according to Maud's descriptions in her books. The designers of

The Macdonalds' home in Toronto was called Journey's End.

Green Gables focused on the way the house would have looked about four years after Anne's arrival there, when she was fully settled in with Matthew and Marilla Cuthbert. Green Gables would be of interest to historians as well as *Anne* fans. Authentically furnished, it was a typical Prince Edward Island farmhouse of the 1890s. There were few of those left, as the farmers of the 1930s renovated their old family homes and added modern conveniences. Stepping into Green Gables would not only be like stepping into the pages of a novel, it would also be like stepping backward in time.

Maud's feelings were mixed about Green Gables becoming part of a park. She was sorry to be losing the property that had belonged to her family. At the same time, however, she was glad that the house would be well cared for. She had not forgotten the sad and haunting experience of walking through her grandmother's house, empty, locked, and untouched for seven years.

Around the same time, something happened to renew interest in Green Gables. Two films had already been made of Maud's first and most famous book. In 1937 the story was produced in still another format. Two different playwrights, Alice Chadwicke and Wilbur Braun, both adapted *Anne of Green Gables* for the stage at the same time. Although she liked Chadwicke's version better, Maud was not satisfied with either of the plays. And, as with the films, she had forfeited her right to any money from dramatic productions.

Meanwhile, Maud was working on the book *Jane of Lantern Hill*. The story was an optimistic one—something Maud's life was *not* while she was writing it. Both Chester and Stuart were now in college. Chester was deciding between careers in mining engineering or law. Stuart was interested in studying medicine. Now that her sons were grown and she no longer had to fulfill the duties of the minister's wife, Maud should have had plenty of time to write. But Ewan's condition had not improved since his retirement. Caring for her husband was wearing Maud down, mentally and physically. The tranquilizers she took to deal with the stresses of her life did her weakened body more harm than good. She had always managed to find the time and energy to write: secretly, behind her teacher's back; in the cold dawn of winter, before setting off to teach at her one-room schoolhouse; in a busy newsroom. Now her energy and drive seemed to be failing; she was getting— and feeling—old. "I admire gray hair—on other people," Maud had once remarked. The gray hair was now hers.

As *Jane of Lantern Hill* neared its publication date, Maud's cat, Good Luck, suddenly died. Maud had owned many cats in her lifetime, and several since her

Ewan's retirement should have given Maud more time for her writing—but it didn't.

marriage. Daffy, the first cat to occupy the Leaskdale manse, had been accidentally shot by a hunter. His successor was Paddy. They had been good pets, but Maud had never loved them the way she loved Good Luck, or Lucky. Maud believed that animals, especially cats, had souls and went to their own heaven when they died. But Good Luck, Maud insisted, had something close to a human soul, for she claimed that she could see it in his intelligent eyes. With difficulties accumulating in her life, Maud was devastated at the death of Good Luck, her beloved companion. *Jane of Lantern Hill* is dedicated, not to a human being, but to Maud's favorite feline: Lucky.

Afterward, she tried to work on a sequel to *Jane of Lantern Hill*, but her heart wasn't in the project. Another war was breaking out in Europe.

Maud had reacted to World War I in very personal terms. Before long, World War II was affecting her in the same way. She followed the news of the war closely, as if she had family in the front lines. And she very nearly did.

Both Chester and Stuart were the right age to join the Canadian armed forces. Being patriotic, both wanted to do their part in the war. Chester volunteered, but he was rejected because he was nearsighted. Stuart, who was studying to be a doctor, wanted to join a medical unit. There was a rule, however, that he could not do this until he finished his studies, so he stayed in college. With Ewan about to go to a clinic in Florida and Maud obviously upset and strained, Stuart didn't want to give his mother one more reason to worry. But he vowed to join the navy as soon as he could.

In 1940 Maud fell and injured her right arm quite badly. She couldn't seem to recover afterward. Around the same time, there was a stretch of bad news about the war. Chester and his new wife were having marital difficulties that would lead to divorce. Ewan's depression and memory loss showed no signs of improving. With events like these on her mind, Maud grew more and more depressed and despondent. She even admitted her despair in letters to Ephraim Weber and George MacMillan—something she had never done before. Her strength and her will to live were failing: Maud was dying.

Maud had once said that her greatest fear was to die a long, lingering death from cancer. The mental and emotional breakdown that she suffered in her final months was not cancer, but its effects were just as slow and agonizing, and its end just as inevitable. On April 24, 1942, at the age of sixty-seven, utterly exhausted from the constant strain of holding her family together and hiding its many private difficulties from prying eyes, Maud died.

She was buried on Prince Edward Island, in the Cavendish graveyard. The same minister who had married Maud and Ewan now officiated at Maud's funeral. At the service, he read aloud from Maud's own writings. Among the readings were a poem from *The Watchman* and excerpts from *Chronicles of Avonlea*.

Two years later, Ewan Macdonald was buried beside his wife.

Maud Montgomery Macdonald had lived a difficult life, blessed and buoyed, until that terrible time at the very end, by what she called "the gift of wings": imagination. Through her writing, she has succeeded in passing the gift on to new generations of readers, young and old.

Chapter 13

Early in their friendship, Ephraim Weber offered to write Maud's biography someday. Maud was aghast at the idea. She felt that biographies simplified a person's life instead of delving into its complexities, good and bad. According to Maud, they never gave a complete and accurate picture of the person. Eventually she changed her mind somewhat. She even gave Weber permission to write and publish an article about her life.

For someone who didn't want her biography written, Maud certainly left an amazingly complete and detailed record of her life. She'd kept all the journals and diaries she'd written since her teenage years. Often she regretted burning the earlier diaries from her childhood, and all those old stories, like "My Graves" and "The History of Flossy Brighteyes."

At the same time that she was writing her novels and raising her family, Maud undertook a huge project. She began editing her old journals, copying the entries neatly into fresh notebooks. After she died, her family placed her journals in the archives at the University of Guelph, near Toronto. The family asked that the notebooks be sealed and locked away until 1992, fifty years after Maud's death. Until then, they were accessible to scholars, but not to the public. There are, however, edited, published versions of the journals up to 1921, with additional volumes anticipated.

Her personal journals may have been locked away until 1992, but Maud's books seem to be everywhere. *Anne of Green Gables* has been translated into languages representing the entire world, including Japanese, Icelandic, Polish, Finnish, and Swedish. It has also been printed in Braille so the blind can enjoy Anne.

Maud's most famous book has delighted readers continuously since it first appeared in 1908. Now it is delighting a variety of viewers as well. During Maud's lifetime, it was produced twice as a film and twice as a play. In 1964 the Confederation Centre Theatre opened in Charlottetown, the capital of Prince Edward Island. The following summer, the theater premiered a new musical dear to the hearts of the Island's inhabitants: *Anne of Green Gables*. The musical's lyrics were written by a Canadian actor, Donald Harron; the music was composed by television director Norman Campbell. The show has been playing to full houses during the Confederation Centre Theatre's summer season ever since.

The musical has also been enjoyed by audiences around the world. In the spring of 1969, *Anne of Green Gables* opened in London, where it played for nearly a year. At the same time, another company was performing the show in Nairobi, the capital of Kenya, in Africa. In 1970 Osaka, Japan, hosted a world's fair, Expo '70. One of the major attractions of Expo '70, playing to a consistently sold-out theater, was *Anne of Green Gables*. New York City is the ultimate goal of most musicals. *Anne of Green Gables* reached that goal for two weeks during the Christmas season in 1971, when it played the City Center Theater. "The character of Anne," one critic said, "remains totally lovable, the kind of girl everyone should invite over for Christmas."

Today most popular books are eventually adapted for television. *Anne of Green Gables* is no exception. In the early 1970s the BBC, England's radio and television broadcasting company, produced two miniseries about Anne. Ten years later, Sullivan Films of Canada also decided to create a television movie based on its country's most popular heroine. Viewers in Canada and the United States were delighted by *Anne of Green Gables* and its sequel, both starring actress Megan Follows. The first film won an Emmy Award for excellence in a program for children. *Jane of Lantern Hill* has also been produced for television.

Now even ballet audiences can enjoy Maud Montgomery's most famous character! Jacques Lemay, a choreographer, took the score Norman Campbell had written for the Charlottetown musical. He created new dances to Campbell's music, dances much more classical in style than those in the original show. Lemay's ballet version of *Anne of Green Gables* was performed by a Canadian company, the Royal Winnipeg Ballet, at Lehman Center for the Performing Arts in the Bronx, New York, in 1989.

Once people have discovered L. M. Montgomery's books, they often want to see the places she describes. Even without its literary connections, Prince Edward Island is a lovely vacation spot. Its only link with mainland Canada is still by boat. The Island has beautiful beaches, a comfortable summer climate, mile upon mile of rural scenery, and a fine cultural center in Charlottetown. Visitors appreciate these things; but for many, it is Maud—and Anne—that they've come to look for. Largely because of L. M. Montgomery, tourism is the Island's second most important industry.

Tourists who come looking for signs of Maud and her books are not disappointed. One of the ferryboats sailing between Prince Edward Island and New Brunswick is called the *Lucy Maud Montgomery*. On the Island itself, Green Gables is, of course, the main attraction. Visitors interested in the author as well as her characters can stop at the house where Maud was born, in nearby New London (formerly known as Clifton). The little house has been turned into an L. M. Montgomery museum. Maud's wedding dress is there, and also a display of the scrapbooks in which she kept her earliest writings. The house at Park Corner where Maud often visited her cousins, including Frede, has

*Green Gables House, Prince Edward Island National Park
(Canadian Parks Service)*

become a museum, too: the Anne of Green Gables Museum at Silver Bush. Maud was married in this house; the organ played for her wedding is still there. So are first-edition copies of many of Maud's books, all autographed. The Macneill homestead where Maud grew up is no longer standing, but its current owners—Macneill descendants—have restored the foundation of the house and the orchard and gardens Maud loved so much.

An amazing proportion of the visitors to Green Gables and Prince Edward Island's other L. M. Montgomery museums are Japanese. Some Japanese couples actually travel the fourteen thousand miles between their island and Maud's island to get married on the grounds of Green Gables! These pilgrimages arise from the popularity of *Anne of Green Gables* among schoolchildren in Japan. They know the book as *Akage No An: Anne of the Red Hair*. For many years, *Anne* has been included as a literature text in Japanese schools. Some people say that Anne appeals so strongly to Japanese children because she has a poetic, imaginative, creative spirit, but at the same time she must try very hard to respect authority, a conflict shared by many Japanese children. Also, Anne's priorities are family and education, things that are valued highly in Japanese culture.

At a time when women were expected to be housewives and mothers, Maud Montgomery aspired, not only to a career, but to a career as a serious writer, a field dominated by men and difficult for anyone. For every successful author, there are dozens who write and write and whose works never become famous, or are never published at all. With the odds of the times against her, Maud Montgomery not only became a writer, she became a successful writer, one whose name was known by children and adults around the world. Her lifetime earnings totaled about $200,000. And, after nearly a century, her books are still read and loved.

In 1947 a Canadian newspaper conducted a survey.

It asked its readers who their favorite authors were. The paper's readers had classic tastes: the number-one favorite was Charles Dickens. But not far behind the immortal Dickens was the woman who, in her youth, wanted "to write a book that will live," and did: Maud Montgomery.

Chapter Notes

INTRODUCTION

xii   "curling breakers . . . flowers" *The Selected Journals of L. M. Montgomery*, Volume 2: 1910–1921, ed. Mary Rubio and Elizabeth Waterston (Toronto: Oxford University Press, 1987), 370.

CHAPTER 1

2   "spelled . . . please." *Journals*, v. 2, 67.

2   "a beautiful, spiritual . . . impulses." *The Selected Journals of L. M. Montgomery*, Volume 1: 1889–1910, ed. Mary Rubio and Elizabeth Waterston (Toronto: Oxford University Press, 1985), 300.

5   "Even yet . . . away." L. M. Montgomery, *The Alpine Path: The Story of My Career* (Markham, Ontario: Fitzhenry and Whiteside, 1917), 17.

6   "I like . . . geraniums." *Journals*, v. 1, 1.

8   "Before . . . soul." *The Green Gables Letters: From L. M. Montgomery to Ephraim Weber 1905–1909*, ed. Wilfred Eggleston (Toronto: Ryerson Press, 1960), 24.

14   "I like . . . spine." *The Alpine Path*, 49.

15   "Were it . . . written." *The Alpine Path*, 52.

CHAPTER 2

18 "She was . . . known." *The Alpine Path*, 16.
19 "in Scripture," *Journals*, v. 1, 376.
21 "Autumn" *The Alpine Path*, 53.
24 "Evening Dreams," *Journals*, v. 1, 259.
24 "very pretty," *Journals*, v. 1, 258.
25 "that people . . . writing." *The Alpine Path*, 56.
26 "I couldn't . . . tribulation." *The Alpine Path*, 58.
27 "The vessel . . . forgotten." Francis W. P. Bolger, *The Years Before "Anne"* (Prince Edward Island Heritage Foundation, 1974), 34.
28 "If you count . . . husband." *Journals*, v. 1, 14.
28 "Life . . . for me." *Journals*, v. 1, 1.

CHAPTER 3

32 "ten-year letters." *Journals*, v. 1, 253.
37 "I heartily . . . Venezuela." *The Years before "Anne*," 97.
39 "This . . . yesterday." *Journals*, v. 1, 35.
40 "kindred spirits." *Journals*, v. 1, 36.

CHAPTER 4

44 "I had . . . all day." *Journals*, v. 1, 116.
46 "No pay . . . some day." *Journals*, v. 1, 140.
49 "People envy . . . travelling." *Journals*, v. 1, 162.
50 "I can *never* . . . *never!*" *Journals*, v. 1, 201.
51 "I could not . . . marry," *Journals*, v. 1, 189–190.
52 "There I was . . . love." *Journals*, v. 1, 212.
52 "It is . . . marry him." *Journals*, v. 1, 123.
54 "of poking . . . purse." *Journals*, v. 1, 252.
55 "the foremost . . . toil." *Journals*, v. 1, 257.

CHAPTER 5

56 "I'm a newspaperwoman!" *Journals*, v. 1, 264.
57 "general handyman." *Journals*, v. 1, 264.
58 "fun . . . fancies." *Journals*, v. 1, 266.
58 "Evidently . . . society." *Journals*, v. 1, 266.
59 "My knowledge . . . queens." *The Alpine Path*, 68.
61 "I hate . . . stuff." *Journals*, v. 1, 279.
62 "Editors . . . them." *Journals*, v. 1, 290.
63 "But only . . . could." *Green Gables Letters*, 87.

CHAPTER 6

67 "I've known . . . heaven." *Green Gables Letters*, 29.
69–70 "It was . . . star." *Journals*, v. 2, 8.
70 "It would . . . suns." Mollie Gillen, *The Wheel of Things: A Biography of L. M. Montgomery* (Markham, Ontario: Fitzhenry and Whiteside, 1975), 97.
70 "God . . . himself." *The Wheel of Things*, 123.
71 "Prayer meeting . . . have." *Journals*, v. 1, 7.

CHAPTER 7

73 "Elderly . . . them." *Journals*, v. 1, 330.
79 "I'm awfully . . . college." *Green Gables Letters*, 74.
80 "My book . . . publishers." *The Alpine Path*, 77.
80 "I don't know . . . edition." *Green Gables Letters*, 73.
83 "the dearest . . . Alice." *Green Gables Letters*, 71.

CHAPTER 8

90 "Maud . . . Macdonald." *Journals*, v. 2, 67.
96 "Really . . . soul." *Green Gables Letters*, 59.
97 "Yes . . . writer." *The Years Before "Anne,"* 201.

CHAPTER 9

102   "May Wilhelm . . . broken!" *Journals*, v. 2, 166.
109   "Those . . . wives." *The Wheel of Things*, 117.
113   "Crass . . . Yankeeism!" *Journals*, v. 2, 373.
114   "I am done . . . now." *Journals*, v. 2, 390.
115   "old gods . . . underworld." *The Wheel of Things*, 139.

CHAPTER 10

118   *"They . . .* cajole." *Journals*, v. 2, 285.

CHAPTER 11

129   "romantic book of the month," *The Wheel of Things*, 179.

CHAPTER 12

135   "I admire . . . people." *Journals*, v. 2, 130.
138   "the gift of wings," *Journals*, v. 2, 369.

CHAPTER 13

141   "The character . . . Christmas." Clive Barnes, "Theater:
Folksy Charms of 'Anne of Green Gables,' " *New York
Times*, Wednesday, December 22, 1971, 30:1.
145   "to write a book that will live." *Journals*, v. 2, 146.

Bibliography

BY L. M. MONTGOMERY

Anne of Green Gables	(1908)
Anne of Avonlea	(1909)
Kilmeny of the Orchard	(1910)
The Story Girl	(1911)
Chronicles of Avonlea	(1912)
The Golden Road	(1913)
Anne of the Island	(1915)
The Watchman and Other Poems	(1916)
Anne's House of Dreams	(1917)
The Alpine Path	(1917)
Rainbow Valley	(1919)
Further Chronicles of Avonlea	(1920)
Rilla of Ingleside	(1921)
Emily of New Moon	(1923)
Emily Climbs	(1925)
The Blue Castle	(1926)
Emily's Quest	(1927)
Magic for Marigold	(1929)
A Tangled Web	(1931)
Pat of Silver Bush	(1933)
Courageous Women	(1934)
(with Marian Keith and Mabel Burns McKinley)	
Mistress Pat	(1935)
Anne of Windy Poplars	(1936)
Jane of Lantern Hill	(1937)
Anne of Ingleside	(1939)

ABOUT L. M. MONTGOMERY

Abley, Mark. "The Girl She Never Was." *Saturday Night* 52 (November 1987): 53–59.

Anderson, Jack. "Royal Winnipeg's 'Anne of Green Gables.' " *New York Times*, 24 October 1989.

Barnes, Clive. "Theater: Folksy Charms of 'Anne of Green Gables,' " *New York Times*, 22 December 1971.

Bolger, Francis W. P., and Elizabeth R. Epperly, eds. *My Dear Mr. M.: Letters to G. B. MacMillan.* Toronto: McGraw Hill Ryerson, 1980.

Bolger, Francis W. P. *The Years Before "Anne."* Prince Edward Island Heritage Foundation, 1974.

Bruce, Harry. *Maud: The Life of L. M. Montgomery.* New York: Bantam, 1992.

Eggleston, Wilfred, ed. *The Green Gables Letters: From L. M. Montgomery to Ephraim Weber 1905–1909.* Toronto: Ryerson Press, 1960.

Gaudet, Charmaine. "Why the Japanese Love Our Anne." *Canadian Geographic* 107 (Feb.–Mar. 1987): 8–15.

Gillen, Mollie. *The Wheel of Things: A Biography of L. M. Montgomery.* Markham, Ontario: Fitzhenry and Whiteside, 1975.

Holzer, Harold. "A Visit to Green Gables." *Americana* 16 (June 1988): 58–63.

Johnson, Brian. "Anne of Green Gables: The Sequel." *Maclean's* 100 (7 December 1987): 46–50.

Rubio, Mary. "Anne of Green Gables: The Architect of Adolescence." In *Touchstones: Reflections of the Best in Children's*

Literature, edited by Perry Nodelman. West Lafayette, Ind.: Children's Literature Association of America, 1985, 173–187.

Rubio, Mary and Elizabeth Waterston, eds. *The Selected Journals of L. M. Montgomery*. Vol. 1: 1889–1910. Toronto: Oxford University Press, 1985.

Rubio, Mary and Elizabeth Waterston, eds. *The Selected Journals of L. M. Montgomery*. Vol. 2: 1910–1921. Toronto: Oxford University Press, 1987.

Russell, D. W., Ruth Russell, and Rea Wilmshurst. *Lucy Maud Montgomery: A Preliminary Bibliography*. Waterloo, Ontario: University of Waterloo Press, 1986.

Shortell, Ann. "An Author's Painful Secrets." *Maclean's* 100 (7 December 1987): 50.

Women's Institute. *Lucy Maud Montgomery, The Island's Lady of Stories*. Springfield, Prince Edward Island: Women's Institute, 1963.

Additional information about L. M. Montgomery and her works can be found in the afterwords by Mary Rubio and Elizabeth Waterston in the New American Library Editions of *Anne of Green Gables* (1987), *Anne of Avonlea* (1987), *Chronicles of Avonlea* (1989), *Anne's House of Dreams* (1989), *The Story Girl* (1990), and *Anne of the Island* (1990). The periodical *CCL: Canadian Children's Literature/Littérature canadienne pour la jeunesse* also frequently prints articles, most scholarly in nature, relating to L. M. Montgomery and her novels.

Index

3